A NICE
MURDER
FOR MOM

A NICE MURDER FOR MOM

James Yaffe

ST. MARTIN'S PRESS
NEW YORK

Design by Glen M. Edelstein

Library of Congress Cataloging-in-Publication Data

Yaffe, James.
    A nice murder for Mom / James Yaffe.
        p.   cm.
    "A Thomas Dunne book."
    ISBN 0-312-02260-3
    I. Title.
    PS3547. A16N54 1988
    813'.54—dc19   88-11584
                                                CIP

First Edition

10 9 8 7 6 5 4 3 2 1

To Robert Freedman, my friend and my agent,
with gratitude for understanding what it's like.

A NICE
MURDER
FOR MOM

PROLOGUE

My darling son Davie,

I'm sitting here in the airplane, flying back to New York, and writing to you this letter. And even while I'm writing it I know I'm not going to send it.

For a couple of days now I'm arguing about this inside myself. Should I tell you the truth, or should I keep it strictly to myself? On the one hand, is it good for my health I should keep it inside myself like a bottle? On the other hand, if I tell you the truth, don't I know what you'll do with it?

So what I decided is, I'll write this all down on paper, get it out of my system, and then I'll throw it away.

What I'm referring to is who killed the professor.

No, it isn't exactly that I told you any lies again. Everything I explained to you two days ago was true. My chain of reasoning didn't have anything wrong with it. It was a beautiful chain of reasoning. But even while I was putting it together, I felt funny about it. I couldn't pretend there weren't a few bits and pieces which just wouldn't fall into place.

What I finally realized is, these bits and pieces don't contradict my earlier conclusions. What they show me is, there are other conclusions, too. The ones I can't ever tell you about.

Probably you could work them out by yourself, if you went over in your mind everything that happened in the last week. . . .

CHAPTER 1

MY MOTHER ALWAYS WANTED me to be a professional man. It didn't matter to her what kind of profession. Any kind would do, as long as it was really "professional," and absolutely not "business."

"Your uncles are in business, your cousins are in business, your father was in business, and none of them ever made a cent of money," Mom always said. "Except your Uncle Max, and he doesn't count, because God forbid you should turn out to be such a physical and nervous wreck as your Uncle Max and your Aunt Selma."

And so, even when I was a small boy in the Bronx, Mom saw to it that I got some professional training. She gave me chemistry sets for my birthday; she made me take violin lessons; on vacations she took me down to the law courts to watch the cases. And finally Mom got her wish. I became a professional man. But I'm afraid this fact never gave her much satisfaction. She didn't exactly expect me to become a policeman.

From the very beginning she raised objections, every day a new objection, but most of them were smoke screens. Her antagonism to the life of a policeman really boiled down to two points. One: The work is dangerous. "All those gangsters and dope fiends and bookies and hatchet murderers and other such goniffs you have to deal with," she said. "Isn't it possible that you could get hurt someday?"

Two: She thought the job was beneath me. "Always it was my ambition that you should take up something that needs a little intelligence and brainpower," she said. "But this detective work, this figuring out who killed who, and playing cops and robbers like the kiddies in the park, this is no work for a grown-up man. For all the brains it takes, believe me, you might as well be in business with your uncles."

And there was simply no way of talking Mom out of this opinion, convincing her of the dignity and difficulty of my profession. Even though I did pretty well for myself, became an inspector by the age of forty—the youngest in anybody's memory—Mom never stopped making fun of me.

And with justice. Because to tell the truth, this cops-and-robbers business *was* child's play—for Mom. Figuring out who killed who *was* an easy job—for Mom. With her ordinary common sense, and her natural talent for seeing into people's motives and never letting herself be fooled by anybody (this talent came from her long experience with large-thumbed butchers and shifty-eyed landlords), Mom was usually able to solve, over the dinner table, crimes that kept the police running around in circles for weeks.

In fact, there were times when I suspected that my chief value to the New York Homicide Squad lay not in the strenuous investigating, manhunting, and third-degreeing I did all week, but in the revealing conversations I had with Mom every Friday night, when she invited my wife, Shirley, and me up to the Bronx for dinner.

Those dinners continued for years, even after the

neighborhood went down and Mom finally agreed to move to Ninety-second Street and West End Avenue. She took all the things from her old apartment with her—the heavy old furniture she'd had since her wedding, the faded family photographs, the tintypes of English landscapes and Roman ruins—and was soon solving my cases for me as neatly as ever, between the matzo ball soup and the apple strudel.

And then, a couple of years ago, everything changed.

My job put me in contact with death practically every day of my life. I thought I was hardened to death, until I found out the truth about myself. Shirley's illness lasted less than four months, and when she died, I turned out not to be so hardened after all.

One of the things that came out of it was, I couldn't go on living in New York. Okay, it wasn't exactly rational, and I kept telling myself the feeling would go away. But it didn't go away, and while I was wondering how I was going to survive with it, the opportunity came along. Like a bolt out of the blue, they say—meaning, I suppose, that God does it for you, as suddenly and arbitrarily as He produces bolts of lightning. If you happen to believe in God.

I'm not sure I do, but I certainly didn't turn up my nose at this bolt, wherever it might have come from.

Five years ago, the NYPD paid my expenses so I could go to a symposium on Investigative Techniques that was held in Mesa Grande, a middle-sized town nestling in the foothills of the Rocky Mountains. A couple of hundred police officers from all over the country gathered for a week at The Richelieu, the big resort hotel on the outskirts of town, and attended lectures and workshops on Fingerprints and Bloodstains, How to Question a Suspect without Offending the Supreme Court, and so on. At night, to tell the truth, a lot of drinking went on.

While I was at this symposium, I met Ann Swenson, a young lawyer who was working as an assistant DA in

5

Mesa Grande. Almost young enough to be my daughter, if Shirley and I had ever been able to have children. We hit it off nicely. We had the same ideas about law enforcement and what it has to do with justice, and we both thought most of the other participants in the symposium were idiots.

In the years since then, we wrote back and forth a few times, and suddenly, a few months after Shirley's death, I got a long-distance call from Ann. She was the public defender in Mesa Grande now—a six-year appointment by the City Council, infinitely renewable—and she'd been holding the job for a few months. She had finally convinced the council to appropriate money so the public defender's office could have an investigator of its own— till now it had been dependent on the DA's investigative staff, which meant that Ann had to do it all herself. She wanted to know if I was interested in the job.

I accepted then and there, over the phone. The salary wasn't nearly what I'd been getting as an inspector in the New York Homicide Squad, but how much money did I need, a man living alone, without a wife?

And it would get me out of New York.

It isn't true that I didn't give a thought to how Mom would feel about it. I gave that a lot of thought. I was the only child Mom ever had, and she was over seventy now. Who would keep her company at dinner on Friday nights? Would she ever get another chance to ask me about my cases and exercise her wits in the manner that made those Friday nights so interesting and enjoyable to her?

So I invited her to come with me. I pointed out to her that there was nothing for her in New York, when you got right down to it. Sure, she had friends from her neighborhood and the synagogue and the bridge group she belonged to, but there was a synagogue out in Mesa Grande, too, and I was sure she'd be able to find plenty

6

of bridge players: With her sociable nature, she would make new friends in no time at all.

And her deepest commitment, after all, had always been to her family. None of whom were left for her back in New York. I was her only family now—just as she was mine. Well, there *were* a few relatives on Shirley's side, but Mom and I had pretty much the same opinion of those people.

Mom thanked me for the invitation and said she'd like very much to visit me someday. Not that she felt any particular enthusiasm about seeing the mountains— "What do we need them for?" she said. "If God had intended that people should climb to the top of things, why did he invent elevators?" On the other hand, she admitted that it might be interesting to find out what cowboys and Indians were like. (I had told her that very few of either species could be found in Mesa Grande, but she chose not to believe me: It was "out West," wasn't it?) She couldn't accept my invitation just yet, she said. She was involved in too many things, she wouldn't be able to find the free time for a while.

I understood what she was feeling. She wasn't ready to turn her back on everything her life had been up to now, even though the most important people in it were gone. Maybe later, I told myself, and got on the plane without looking back.

For the next year or so, at regular monthly intervals, I issued my invitation to her all over again. Even if she wouldn't settle with me for good, would she at least come out for a few weeks and pay me a visit? She always thanked me and turned me down.

And then, a few months ago, one morning early in March, Mom called me up long distance.

"So, Davie," she said, "if the invitation is still open, I'll come to visit you like you asked. You're sure you've got an extra bathroom?"

7

"I promise you, Mom."

"And you keep it clean, I hope?"

"It's spotless. I've got a cleaning woman who comes in once a week."

"I can imagine what kind of cleaning women you get out there. All right, don't worry about it. Once I'm there, I'll give her a talking-to. I'm taking an airplane, you can be at the airport to meet me? If you can't, I'll take the airport bus."

"I'll pick you up in my car, Mom. There *is* no airport bus."

"You don't have buses? Let me take a guess. You don't even have a subway, am I right?" I could hear one of her deep exasperated sighs, undiminished by long distance. "All right, I'll see you four o'clock tomorrow afternoon."

"You're coming *tomorrow?*"

"Why not? You're too busy? You've got an important case?"

"Not at all. In fact, it's a perfect time for you to come, things are a little slow just now. But I'm surprised, you seem to have decided so suddenly."

"If I didn't decide suddenly, I wouldn't have decided. So what's the weather like out there? I should pack my flannel underwear? I should buy galoshes?"

"Well, we did have a snowstorm a few days ago. But it's mostly melted now. Actually, it's been a very mild winter, it never gets as cold and nasty here as it does in New York."

Her snort was the quintessence of disbelief. "I'll pack the underwear," she said. "Galoshes I can buy in this town of yours, I suppose. What's the name of it again?"

"Mesa Grande."

"What is that, some kind of foreign name?"

"It's Spanish, Mom."

"The people in the stores talk English though, don't they?"

8

"Oh yes, their accent is pretty thick, of course, but once you get used to it you'll be able to understand every word."

Another snort, but friendlier. "You didn't change much in a year, I notice. Just as fresh to your mother as ever."

She hung up, and I thought how nice it would be to see her. Only one thing worried me. I didn't know how I was going to keep her amused and occupied during her visit. Mesa Grande doesn't offer all that much for the tourist from the big city.

What was needed, of course, to make Mom's vacation a total pleasure for her, was a murder. A nice complicated one, full of twists and turns, the type of murder Mom really loved.

CHAPTER
2

WHICH BRINGS ME TO the night before Mom's arrival, which also happened to be the night before the murder.

I had a date that night. I don't go out too often. Just enough to keep the pressure down, if you know what I mean. I'm not ready yet for anything more serious, and who knows if I'll ever be? My attitude is, if it happens, it'll happen, and meanwhile I'm not worrying about it.

The woman I had the date with was Marcia Lewis, who was co-owner of a local ski-equipment shop. She was in her late thirties, a dozen or so years younger than me, with a divorce behind her and a six-year-old daughter. She was a brunette with a nice slim figure that she works at hard, but what I liked best about her was, she was easygoing, she wasn't full of ideas and opinions that she had to argue about, in company she didn't do much talking but she did do a lot of listening, and she laughed at my jokes.

Maybe it sounds funny that somebody like Marcia should be attractive to me. After all, I was married to

Shirley for twenty-five years, a woman who had a psychology degree from Wellesley and always kept up with the latest developments in the field, even though she never used her degree professionally. The only explanation I can think of is that Marcia agreed with me about keeping the pressure down. For example, we got together for our date one night a week. Regular, like clockwork, every Tuesday we could depend on each other. But never any more than that. On other nights we felt no temptation to see each other, and except to work out the time and place for Tuesday, we didn't call each other up on the phone.

Tonight we were planning to take in a poetry reading at Mesa Grande College, the small undergraduate liberal arts school located in our town. That may not sound like the most exciting way to spend an evening, but Marcia loves poetry. She shows this love not by analyzing it but by clasping her hands together and making little sighing noises. She likes her poetry to rhyme and have what she calls "a lot of rhythm" in it.

Before the reading we had dinner at Pasquale's Pasta Paradise, which is a lot of cuts below half a dozen places I can think of in Little Italy, but it's the best Mesa Grande can offer. While we ate, Marcia told me about the customers who had come into the ski shop that day, and I told her about my exploits in the public defender's office. She responded to them with her eyes wide and lots of interpolated "Goshes" and "Gollys" and "Wows." So I was in a good mood when we finished dinner and drove up to the college in my little 1978 Ford two-door, which is noisy, uncomfortable, and gas-guzzling, but we suit each other.

It was dark out when we reached the campus. I could still see the shreds of last week's snow, clinging to the sparse brown grass. Spring would be along in a month or so, but in this section of the world winter always uses the month of March to give us a few last-minute surprises.

11

The building we were heading for, home of the Humanities Division and the theater auditorium, was Llewellyn Hall, the college's newest gift from a grateful alumnus. A huge square block of concrete, with tiny windows: exactly the same, in its architectural style, as every new office complex, condominium, and prison all over the world.

Poetry readings seldom bring the public out of the bars and grills. A small crowd was gathered outside the auditorium, waiting for the doors to open. Among the assembled poetry lovers, I spotted Mike Russo, who taught American literature with an emphasis on poetry.

Our friendship is an unlikely one. He's twenty-five years younger than I am, pushing twenty-nine, tall and thin and dark, with his hair always unruly and his chin always looking slightly unshaven. The only bond between us—but it's enough—is that we're a couple of transplanted New Yorkers. We met for the first time a year ago at the grand opening in one of the new shopping malls of an establishment that advertised itself as "a genuine New York delicatessen." It turned out to be no such thing: Any deli chef who did what those clowns did to a pastrami would be run out of New York on a rail. But in our annoyance, Mike and I discovered our common bond, and we had kept up an intermittent friendship ever since.

Mike always had a slightly gloomy look on his face—I think it came less from his temperament than from the permanent arch of his thick black eyebrows—but tonight it seemed to me he looked even gloomier than usual.

"Are you okay?" I asked, after disposing of the amenities and introducing him to Marcia. "You look as if you're coming down with something."

"I am," he said. "It's a disease called life."

"When you get to be my age," I said, "you'll understand that the only cure for it is a lot worse than the symptoms."

Mike allowed only the faintest flicker of a smile to pass over his face.

"How about having lunch with me this week?" I said. I was making the suggestion to give him a chance to pour his troubles into a sympathetic ear. Also, I was curious about what was eating him. You don't choose a career as a detective without a certain natural nosiness.

"I'd love to," he said. "But I'm bogged down with committee meetings this week. Listen, do you have any nights free?"

Before I could answer, a voice broke into our conversation. "Oh, God, why do I keep going to these things? If there's anything on earth I hate, it's a poetry reading!"

The voice belonged to a small, sharp-faced young woman who wore thick glasses and no makeup but wasn't completely unsexy either. Mike introduced her as Samantha Fletcher, "our medievalist in the English department."

"That means I teach medieval literature," she said. "It doesn't mean I've got a medieval mind. For instance, I've *never* particularly enjoyed wearing a hair shirt. So what the hell am I *doing* here tonight?"

"Well, what are you?" Mike said. "You certainly didn't have to come."

"Oh, didn't I? The place is crawling with spies. If the word got around I *didn't* come, don't you think I wouldn't hear about it when my tenure decision comes up? 'That Fletcher woman—yes, she does have a certain scholarly competence in her field, but she has no community spirit, never supports the cultural events on campus, and incidentally, did you realize she's completely insensitive to poetry?'"

I thought I saw Mike tighten up, as if he were giving a wince of pain.

"Will you be at the great man's tomorrow night?" Samantha Fletcher said.

"I haven't decided yet," Mike said.

"Well, you won't catch *me* staying away. They say he keeps a little grade book next to his bed table, and if you don't show up, he puts an absent mark after your name." She turned to Marcia and me. "Only joking, of course. I was talking about the party our department chairman is giving tomorrow. Once a month or so he has these get-togethers for his minions."

The auditorium doors were opened, and the audience started filing in. "This shouldn't be too bad," Mike said. "I've read some of his stuff in the little magazines, and he's actually got something to say."

"Will his poems have rhymes in them?" Marcia asked.

But before anyone could answer her, a new voice entered the conversation.

"If *you* recommend him, Michael, he's got to be good, doesn't he?"

It was a deep drawling voice, with a sarcastic edge to it, and it came out of a blond giant, about Mike's age, with broad shoulders and a big chest. I recognized his outfit—a brownish tweed sport jacket and a green shirt, open at the collar—as coming from Willingham's, the most expensive clothing store in town.

"Excuse me," he said, turning his smile, frosty and slightly bored, in my direction, "college professors have no manners, do they? So I'll just have to introduce myself. I'm Stuart Bellamy. I teach in the English department, I'm the other American literature nut, along with Michael here. We've met before, haven't we? I seem to recognize you."

I recognized him, too—not because we had met before, which we hadn't, but because his type, smoothly polished by the best prep schools, the most prestigious colleges, and the most impeccable family connections, has given me a pain in the ass all my life. And why is it they're always so *blond*? For a man to be as blond as this Bellamy was strikes me as positively obscene.

I introduced Marcia and myself to him, and he raised

14

an eyebrow at me. "A policeman? I'm impressed. One doesn't think of our stalwart men in blue going in for poetry recitals. Some of the stuff we get exposed to at these affairs *ought* to be criminal offenses, I admit."

Of course, he didn't wait for me to respond to his snotty crack about policemen. People like this Bellamy don't make cracks to be responded to, simply to be heard.

He swung back to Mike Russo and Samantha Fletcher. "Now what were you saying about our star performer tonight, Michael? You can personally vouch for the quality of his *oeuvre*? Well, that's good enough for me. I can't decipher most of this contemporary stuff myself, but fortunately you're always around to explain it to me. Is it because you have that kind of tortuous Mediterranean mind? I really wonder how we'd ever get along here without you."

Bellamy laughed and put his hand, in a gesture of casual affection, on Mike's arm. Mike jerked his arm away.

"Stuart, dear," said Samantha Fletcher, "why don't you try not to be any more of an asshole than usual."

Bellamy chose to take this as a joke, and his hearty laugh rang out. Then he sailed ahead of us into the auditorium—he obviously had a lot of experience sailing ahead of people—and as we followed him, I saw Mike Russo's face. He was staring straight at Bellamy's back, and there was no mistaking that look. Hatred, pure, raw hatred.

It never fails to give me a shock. You don't see it all that often.

The poet who read to us turned out to be an Englishman, wearing rumpled tweeds and speaking in a croaking voice much lubricated with alcohol. I couldn't understand more than every third word of his poetry. As we left, Marcia said to me, just a little forlornly, "Did you hear any rhymes?"

Her complaint went straight to my heart. In a short time we would go back to my house—we couldn't use hers because of her child—and I would do my very best to cheer her up.

Then I felt a hand on my arm and turned to see Mike Russo, looking at me with an expression of great urgency. "Meet me at the party tomorrow night, will you, Dave? It's an open house. Marcus Van Horn—he's the chairman of the English department—always says we can bring people along if we want to. I probably have to make an appearance for an hour or so, but we can go out for a drink afterward."

"Anything particular you want to talk about?"

"I need your advice." He looked around quickly, moved his face closer to mine, and lowered his voice. "You've got a lot of experience with murders, don't you?"

"I'm afraid I do."

"I think I'm on the verge of committing one," he said. "You have to tell me how I can stop myself."

CHAPTER 3

THE NEXT AFTERNOON I went to meet Mom's plane.

It got in on time, and I ran toward her as she came off the ramp, carrying a battered old cloth suitcase. I was surprised, as I always am when I see Mom after a long absence, at how small she is. This little gray-haired old lady, with the bony wrists and wrinkled face, invariably swelled up in my imagination when I was away from her.

I took her in my arms, and her hug, I noticed, was quick and brisk, as it has always been. This is very nice, it seemed to say, and naturally we love each other, but life is short, so let's not waste too much time on sentimental foolishness.

She broke away from me and swiveled her eyes around, taking in the airport lobby. "It's a real airport, isn't it?" she said. "Not so big as LaGuardia, but definitely up-to-date."

"Oh, yes, we're very proud of it," I said. "Next year they're going to install lights, so the planes can come in at night."

17

We moved up the ramp and walked down the stairs to the baggage claim. Luckily Mom's suitcase showed up on the conveyor belt. If it hadn't, I could imagine what she would have had to say about efficiency out here in the middle of nowhere.

I carried her suitcase across the airport parking lot to my trusty little Ford. Mom gave it a sour look. "You drive this thing slowly, don't you?"

"I'll stay under the speed limit, Mom."

She lifted her eyebrows. "You can get it to go over?"

It's a fifteen-minute drive back to town, and you're pointed toward the mountains all the way. Mom was silent for a long time, leaning forward a little, staring ahead through the windshield. Finally she said, "The big one, the one that's sticking up over the others—it's got a name?"

I told her. She grunted and said she had heard of it.

"It's pretty impressive, isn't it?" I asked.

"It's nice," she said. "It'll never beat the Empire State Building, but I wouldn't knock it."

"Some people prefer it to the Empire State Building," I said. "Because God made it."

"That's a reason? Who do they think made the Empire State Building? New Yorkers did. And didn't God make New Yorkers?"

"A lot of people out here aren't so sure of that."

"They don't like New Yorkers out here?"

"Let's just say they've got their own way of doing things in this part of the country, and they think it's superior to New York's way."

Mom sighed, as if she could hardly believe that such ignorance still existed in the world. Then she turned away from the mountains and started looking out the sides of the car.

The ride from the airport to downtown Mesa Grande is dotted with hideous jerry-built housing developments, most of which have sprung up in the last four or five

18

years. Everybody wants to move out to our section of the country these days, and the local real-estate developers, who have our town firmly in their claws, are not about to dilute their profits with any schemes for sensible growth planning. "Don't Californicate Our State," say a lot of bumper stickers that you can see around town. But when our local developers smell money to be made, they would gladly fornicate their own children and mothers.

"This is the kind of house you live in?" Mom said.

I assured her that I lived in one of the older sections of town, where the houses were very nice and didn't look as if they would collapse at the first angry word from the mortgage-and-loan company.

We reached downtown, where the oldest and nicest stores in Mesa Grande are located. Naturally it's fighting a desperate battle right now, in competition with the shopping malls that have popped up like fistulas to the east and north of town.

"This is the main drag," I said. "It's got some very nice places for shopping, I'll bring you down here tomorrow morning if you want. It's not Fifth Avenue, of course."

"If the prices also aren't Fifth Avenue, that could be a good thing," she said.

We went through downtown, no building higher than four stories and the same parade of stores—Woolworth's, Rexall Drugs, Florsheim Shoes, etc.—that you find on any Main Street in any middle-sized city in America. Leave it to Mom, though, to notice the peculiar twist that the parade takes in Mesa Grande. "A lot of windows with rifles in them," she said. "People go in for killing each other around here?"

"No more so than in New York," I said. "The guns you see are mostly so people can kill animals. Deer, pheasants, ducks, an occasional bear. In the same stores

19

you'll find fishing gear, skis, climbing equipment—around here people like to get up into the mountains."

"Who can blame them? How else are they going to get away from the town?"

Downtown was behind us now—it didn't take long to get through it—and we were driving through the older residential section of town. Wide old streets lined with trees and modest frame houses: residential area, middle grade. Then into another residential area—upper-middle grade: larger houses, higher hedges blocking them off from the outside world.

Finally the houses got smaller and the hedges lower: We were in my own neighborhood. I pulled up in front of my house, which is painted white, with green shutters, in a style much closer to New England than to the Southwest. Why was I feeling so nervous? Why should I care if Mom liked it or not? I'd been living in it contentedly for over a year, the first house I'd ever owned in my life.

Mom got out of the car and stood at the end of my front walk for what seemed like a long time, her eyes scrunched together, peering hard. At last she gave a nod.

"At least it's all right on the outside," she said.

I was relieved. My house met with Mom's approval: I wouldn't have to raze it and start over again.

I won't go into detail about what happened when we went inside. I had known the interior would fall below her standards, and it did. Her comments on my carpets, my furniture, my drapes, my plumbing, and the size and shape of my rooms will go unrecorded. She was obviously having the time of her life.

She ended up by dashing into the kitchen and flinging open the refrigerator door. "So let's see what you've got for dinner!"

"For God's sake, Mom, you don't have to cook dinner tonight. I thought I'd take you out somewhere."

"This town has restaurants?"

"Well, of course—"

"What salary do they pay you, working for the public offender?"

I told her, and she made a humphing noise. "On your salary we're not going to any restaurants. All those fast foods, I can imagine how you've been ruining your stomach the last year. That's one thing I can do for you while I'm here, I can at least feed you up and keep the ulcers away for another few years. This is it? This is what you keep in the icebox for eating? It's too late for the supermarkets, I suppose? All right, I'll do what I can. At least you heard about eggs."

She shooed me out of the kitchen fast, and for the next hour I could hear pots banging and plates clinking, and Mom accompanying it all with a tuneless humming. Out of all this came a cheese omelette, a quick delectable reminder of what I'd been missing.

After dinner, we settled in the living room, where Mom found a chair—an old rocker, with chintz covering—that she admitted was "fairly comfortable." I told Mom I was meeting a friend at a party given by one of the professors at the college. Come to think of it, why didn't Mom come with me?

"It's a female friend?" Her eyes lit up with a familiar gleam I hadn't seen for years. "Somebody you're serious about?"

"If what you mean is, are there any future plans—it's just not the direction of my thinking right now."

"Thinking, he calls it! It isn't healthy a man your age living alone. It's terrible for the drapes and the carpets."

"As it happens, Mom, the person I'm meeting tonight is male, not female. He's got some kind of problem, and he needs a pair of sympathetic ears. I'm sure he'd be grateful for two pairs."

"It's nice of you to ask, thank you for the invitation. But tonight I'll go to bed early. It's two hours later in New York, already my bedtime. Have fun at your party,

21

Davie. It's a professor who's giving it? So there wouldn't be any heavy drinking or smoking pot, I suppose."

"You'd be surprised what these academic types get up to nowadays," I said.

Before I left the house, I gave Mom a hug and told her how happy I was she had come. She responded with one of her humphing sounds.

CHAPTER 4

MARCUS VAN HORN, the chairman of the Mesa Grande College English department, lived in one of the more expensive neighborhoods in town. He had money over and above his salary, or at least his late wife had had it.

His whole house was lit up, and cars were lined up on both sides of the street: I had to park around the corner. Party noises came from inside as I moved up the front steps: laughter, talking, but no loud rock music, which was a dead giveaway to what generation the host belonged to.

The front door was wide open, and I stepped into a foyer packed with people and thick with smoke. In this crush I might easily have got through the whole evening without encountering my host, but as luck would have it he was standing only a few feet away from me. I knew him from a case I had worked on when I first got to town. (Ann had defended one of the college janitors, accused of stealing computers from the classrooms. She got him off when I dug up evidence that the guilty party was the technician who had installed those computers in the first place.) With his round face, his wispy gray mustache, his terribly genteel English-professor purr, Van Horn reminded me of a cat. A sixtyish, kind of decadent cat.

I introduced myself to him, and he said, "How nice to see you again! How nice of you to come!"

"Mike Russo asked me to drop in tonight," I said. "He said it was an open house—"

"It certainly is! I welcome unexpected guests, especially members of the local community, I believe it's vitally important to bring the town and the gown together. I don't think Mike has arrived yet—at least he wasn't here ten or fifteen minutes ago, the last time I looked. I'm sure he'll be along shortly, it's after seven-thirty, come in and have a drink, won't you? Right through this archway—if you can fight your way over to the table. There's sherry, and of course my hot rum punch. I'm rather famous on campus for my hot rum punch."

He ran interference for me to his living room, which looked huge even though it was full of chattering college professors. Polished brass, leather bindings, finished wood: pretentious coziness.

Sherry is one drink that I really can't stand, so I settled for the hot rum punch. It was pretty hot.

"Well, how are things in the public defender's office?" Van Horn said. "Any exciting cases these days? Any innocent men you're about to snatch from the shadow of the death house?"

"As a matter of fact," I began, but I never got the chance to finish the brilliantly witty response I was about to make. Unfortunately, it's completely slipped my mind by now.

"Good heavens, we're running out of punch!" Van Horn cried. "I must pop into the kitchen and whip up another batch—the secret, you know, is the cinnamon

24

and cloves—" And I hardly had time to close my mouth when he was gone.

For the next few minutes I made my way aimlessly through the crowd, balancing my glass with the hot rum in it while I also attempted to wolf down some slivers of cheese.

"We meet again!"

I turned around and found myself looking into the spectacled face of Samantha Fletcher, the medievalist I had met at last night's poetry reading. "Two academic gatherings in a row," she said. "And you don't even work at the college! You must be some kind of masochist."

"I'm supposed to meet Mike Russo here," I said.

"Isn't he here yet? I just got here myself. I hope he arrives soon, because I'm very anxious to finish up an argument the two of us got into last night, after the poetry reading. About deconstructionism and fascism. We were both too tired to really dig into the subject."

She plunged into the details of that argument, but it not only didn't interest me, I couldn't understand half the words she used. Will somebody tell me please what a "text" is? Don't people read plays and poems and stories anymore, the way they used to do when *I* was in college? Then I heard the phone ring.

It was in the foyer, I noticed, on a little spindly legged mahogany table. An expensive item, I would've guessed. The phone rang three or four times, with everybody closest to it blandly ignoring it. One of the things in this world I can't stand is an unanswered phone, so I turned away from Fletcher—my rudeness not bothering her a bit: She went right on with her monologue, directing it at somebody who had just come up on her left—and went out to the foyer and picked up the receiver.

I said hello and started to say "Professor Van Horn's residence," but the person at the other end interrupted me. "Stu Bellamy here," he said. "Samantha Fletcher, please."

I recognized that irritating drawling voice from last night, but I saw no point in identifying myself. I just said, "I'll go get her, just a minute," and put the receiver down. Then I went back as far as the archway and signaled to Fletcher inside the living room. "It's Professor Bellamy on the phone, he wants to talk to you."

"But I'd heard he was sick in bed with the flu," Fletcher said. "That's why he isn't here tonight. Why on earth is he calling *me*?"

She headed for the foyer, and I headed after her, and when she picked up the receiver I was right next to her, squeezed pretty close to her by the press of people, so I could make out what Bellamy was saying at the other end of the line.

Why *should* I have made out anything? somebody might ask. What business was it of mine to stand there and listen in on somebody else's conversation? The answer is, there was something about the look on Fletcher's face that roused my curiosity, and once my curiosity is roused I have to unrouse it or I'll go around in a lousy mood for days.

And I wasn't the only nosy one in the place. Marcus Van Horn got to that phone around the same time I did, shoving his face as close to the receiver as he could, while his little cat's eyes glittered.

Fletcher got on the line and said, "It's Samantha, what do you want, Stu?"

Bellamy didn't answer for a second or two, as if he was uncertain if he wanted to go on with the conversation or not, and then he said, "All right, Samantha, you win. Here's the last paragraph of *Black Boy*."

And then he started reading this long passage from a book. I didn't recognize it at the time—since then I've found out it was the last paragraph of the autobiography that Richard Wright wrote back in the 1940s about his childhood down South. And I can quote the paragraph from memory now, because I went over it about a hundred times in the week that followed. It goes like this:

With ever watchful eyes and bearing scars, visible and invisible, I headed North, full of a hazy notion that life could be lived with dignity, that the personalities of others should not be violated, that men should be able to confront other men without fear or shame, and that if men were lucky in their living on earth they might win some redeeming meaning for their having struggled and suffered here beneath the stars.

All the time Bellamy was reading this out, Fletcher was getting more and more excited. The look on her face was positively triumphant. She kept saying things like, "You see what I mean? *Men* should confront other *men!*" But Bellamy paid no attention to any of this, he just kept on reading to the end.

And then, all of a sudden—the moment after he got out the last word, "stars"—we heard this noise. Like a thud or a bang, very loud but also thick, muffled. And then a kind of gasp, or maybe a groan. And then silence.

Fletcher waited a second, then she said, "Stu, what is it? What's going on?" She said his name a few more times, she jiggled the receiver, still no Bellamy. Van Horn said something about a bad connection and the disgraceful telephone service nowadays, so Fletcher hung up the phone and dialed Bellamy's number. This time there was a busy signal.

Van Horn said he'd call the police, and I decided I *was* the police, in a way, so I'd better get out there to Bellamy's house.

Fletcher had turned very white, but she was keeping hold of herself, keeping calm. I asked her if she knew where Bellamy lived, and she said she did, and if I was going to drive out there she'd be glad to show me the way.

By this time Van Horn had contacted headquarters, and they told him they were sending a squad car out to Bellamy's place. But Fletcher and I got on our coats and left the house anyway.

CHAPTER 5

ALL THE WAY OUT to Stuart Bellamy's house, Fletcher sat next to me in my car, with her eyes on the windshield and her hands squeezed together in her lap.

I asked her about the phone call Bellamy had just made to her. What was it all about anyway?

She answered abruptly, her mind obviously not on her words. "We got into a fight last week, Stu and me—and Mike Russo was there, too. About sexism in literature. I expressed the opinion that all books by male writers, even the most well meaning, are essentially sexist. Stu claimed that this book by Richard Wright, *Black Boy,* is an exception. Stu is an authority on black American literature, he's written a lot of articles about it, he's got a big collection of first editions. I challenged him to prove his point, and he said he'd phone me as soon as he'd dug up the passage he had in mind. Tonight he phoned."

She snapped her mouth shut, and for the rest of the twenty-five-minute drive, she didn't say another word.

Bellamy's house was on Blackhawk Road—which

strictly speaking is inside the town limits but hardly seems to be a part of the town at all. It's off to the west, away from any of the shopping centers or thickly populated residential areas. Mesa Grande's been growing like an octopus the last few years, but somehow the growth has slid around Blackhawk Road. Between the houses, which are old and dilapidated, it's got empty lots clogged with weeds. And plenty of snow. Actually our last snow was a week before, but the city fathers of Mesa Grande weren't about to break out the snowplows for the benefit of a neighborhood that has practically no tax-paying citizens in it.

Bellamy's house was as old as all the others in the neighborhood. One of those old-fashioned sprawling giants with porches and catwalks and railings around the roof. But there was nothing dilapidated about it. You could tell he had put a lot of money into it—the paint job was new, the hedges were trimmed, none of the fence posts were falling down, and the front walk was cleared of snow. He must have paid someone to do it. On the basis of my quick look at him the night before, I couldn't see him out there shoveling snow himself.

Fletcher and I got out of the car and started up the front porch. All the lights were on inside, but the shades were down, I couldn't see through the windows. I rang the front doorbell, four or five times, and there was no answer. I tried the doorknob, the door was locked. As a matter of fact, I have a way of dealing with that problem—a certain bunch of keys that I always carry with me—but just then there was a police siren, and a few seconds later a squad car pulled up behind my car, and two uniformed cops got out.

They yelled at us, not very friendly. I think they thought we were in the process of *leaving* the house instead of just getting there. But we identified ourselves, and they calmed down.

They went to the door, too, and it wouldn't open for

them any more than it had for me. One of them went around to the back, while the rest of us waited on the porch. A few minutes later the front door was opened from the inside; the cop had found a window in back that wasn't shut all the way.

We all went into the inside hallway. It was huge, as big as any of the bedrooms in my own house. The floor had an Oriental rug on it, and there was a table with a tall fat vase on it, blue and green, some kind of Chinese design. I don't know anything about that sort of thing, but I would've taken bets it was worth a lot of money.

The two cops led the way through the archway into the living room. The first thing that hit me about that room was the books. There were hundreds of them, covering two walls and stretching up to the ceiling. And there were piles of them on the floor, they seemed to be overflowing from the shelves. And then, in between some of those piles of books, I saw the body. Bellamy's body.

He was lying on the floor, on his stomach, and one of his legs was twisted under him. There was blood on the floor, around his head, and you didn't have to be a doctor to see he was dead. The blood was still wet though, he hadn't turned stiff yet, he couldn't have been dead very long. Fletcher gave a little gasp, I could tell she was on the verge of getting sick, so the officers told her she could go outside. But she wasn't to leave the premises, she had to wait on the front porch.

I can't say I blamed her much. To tell you the truth, I wasn't feeling too great myself. I've had a lot of experience with it, but I still haven't got used to it.

I thought I'd better hang around, though, and see what I could see, just in case this murder should come across Ann Swenson's desk in the next day or two.

The first item I saw, once I was able to tear my eyes away from the body, was the telephone. It was on the floor, as if it had fallen there, maybe a foot or two away from Bellamy's head. The receiver was off the hook.

31

The next item I saw was the book, presumably the one he was reading over the phone just before that thud and that gasp. He was holding it in his right hand, holding onto it tight, as if he wasn't going to let anybody grab it away from him. That's why it was hard to tell just what it was. But I could see the cover had a black background with red letters on it, and a picture of a black man, staring out at the reader. Accusingly.

The next item I saw, lying on the floor next to the body, was a brownish-yellowish object, heavy-looking, probably made of bronze. It seemed to be a kind of paperweight, and it was in the shape of a book. An open book. Both cops headed straight for it, which kept me from getting too good a look at it, but I could see it had smears on it. I was sure they were blood and hairs.

I forced my eyes back to the body, and saw the red torn place behind the left ear. Unless the autopsy came up with something very unusual, it was pretty obvious that somebody had hit Bellamy on the back of his head. Just once was my guess, but enough to do the job.

We all stayed in that house another half hour or so, until a contingent of uniformed police plus plainclothes detectives plus experts with photographic equipment and fingerprinting equipment and so on arrived. Then the scene of the crime was sealed up, and Samantha Fletcher and I were told to drive straight back to Van Horn's house. And just so we wouldn't take any detours along the way, those two uniformed cops climbed in their squad car and followed us.

Three or four detectives from the DA's office had already arrived at Van Horn's house when we got there. They were questioning people one by one in the kitchen, while the rest of Van Horn's guests milled around in the living room and the hallway. Lots of excited buzzing was going on, and Fletcher and I, of course, became the life of the party as soon as we stepped into the house. We

32

had to go over our story again and again. Van Horn was especially insistent on our filling him in on every detail.

Then I saw Mike Russo at the other end of the room. I broke off my narrative—which I was going through for the fifth time, to an entirely new audience—and pushed my way through the crowd to Mike.

"Where've you been?" I said. "Weren't you supposed to meet me here at seven-thirty?"

"I'm sorry, Dave. The craziest thing happened. I overslept. I just lay down for a quick nap after dinner, and the next thing I knew— Well, I didn't actually get here till about half an hour ago. Is it true? Is Stu Bellamy really—?"

I told him it was true all right, and I tried to keep the question that was in my mind from showing on my face. I guess I didn't do too good a job, because Mike suddenly turned a little pale.

"Listen, Dave," he said, "I have to explain to you. That crazy thing I said to you after the reading last night—I was upset about something, I didn't know what I was saying—"

At that moment Mike's name was called out. It was his turn to be questioned by the detectives in the kitchen.

They let him go a little later, and I didn't see him for the rest of the night.

My turn came shortly afterward, and I told them exactly what had happened. I told them three times, in fact, and then they let me go, too.

CHAPTER 6

I GOT HOME A few minutes after midnight. As I stepped into the living room, Mom said, "It was a nice party, I hope?"

In spite of what she had said about New York being two hours later than here, Mom was wide awake. She was sitting in the chintz-covered rocker, and the only light in the room was the standing lamp behind her. She had a copy of *Newsweek* open on her lap.

I was fifty-three years old and hadn't lived at home for thirty-five of them, and my mother was waiting up for me!

But I controlled my impulse to get annoyed at her and said, "Terrific, if what you're looking for in a party is that it should end up in a murder."

I could see Mom's eyes light up with curiosity, but she put on a casual tone. "You're looking exhausted, you want a nice cup of cocoa? I can fix it for you in two minutes."

"I'd prefer a shot of Scotch, after what I've been through tonight."

"I can fix that, too. How do you like it, ice, soda, what?"

"Mom, you're the guest," I said, "you don't have to—"

"A man comes home needing a drink, somebody's got to give it to him. Am I one of these female libbies?"

As she bustled around, putting glass, whiskey, soda, and ice together—she hadn't been in the house twenty-four hours, but already she seemed to know where everything was kept—she said, "Besides, you'll pay me back by telling me about this murder."

As a matter of fact, I didn't need any bribing. I told her everything that had happened to me at the party and afterward.

"Very interesting." Mom settled back in the rocker. "So what's your theory what happened?"

I had no trouble recognizing that innocent look on her face. I remembered it from the old days, whenever she was coaxing me into crawling out on a limb so that she could saw it off. But I started crawling anyway. I've never been able to stop myself.

"It all seems pretty straightforward, Mom. While Bellamy was talking on the phone, somebody sneaked into the house, maybe through the window he left open in the back—some burglar maybe, or somebody who had a grudge against him—and this person came up behind him and hit him over the head." She just kept on smiling at me. I fidgeted a little and said, "I think that's the line the cops are taking, too. What's wrong with it anyway?"

"How can *I* tell you? I'm no policeman, I don't know from murder investigations. If I happen to notice a little hole or two, maybe it's only my imagination."

"What little holes do you happen to notice?"

"For instance—did the murder weapon belong to Professor Bellamy?"

"Yes, it did. Bellamy always kept it on the desk in his living room, everybody who ever visited him noticed it.

35

Besides, who else but a college professor would own a paperweight in the shape of a book?"

"So this burglar, or whoever it is that came up behind him and took him by surprise, wouldn't such a person, such a premeditated killer, bring his own weapon with him? Would he depend on finding a convenient paperweight when the time came? And if he *was* such a *schlimazl* that he forgot to bring a weapon with him, how come he didn't attract Bellamy's attention when he stopped at the desk to pick up the paperweight? In which case Bellamy would've turned around to see who was there, and he wouldn't have been hit on the back of the head."

"Okay, maybe the murderer *didn't* sneak into the house. Maybe Bellamy let him—or her—in himself, and they were talking, and then Bellamy decided to make that phone call, which meant he had to turn his back on the murderer, and that's when the murderer picked up the paperweight and killed him."

Mom gave her head a shake. "If it happened that way, this Bellamy and his murderer are *both schlimazls*. Would Bellamy break off in the middle of a conversation with somebody so he could make a phone call—especially since there was nothing urgent about it? And would this moron murderer decide to kill a man while he's talking on the phone? So in case the man didn't die instantly, he might have time to say the murderer's name to the party at the other end of the line? It's a pretty impatient murderer that wouldn't at least wait until Bellamy was off the phone."

"Maybe he panicked," I said. "Or she. People don't always use logic when they're committing a murder. In any case, Mom, this murder really isn't any of my business. It's up to the police to solve it."

"If they arrest somebody," Mom said, "isn't there a chance your office will be handling the case?"

"Depends on how much money the defendant has.

The people we defend can't afford anybody else. We're the last resort, the bottom of the barrel."

We both started yawning then, so we had to break off the session. Mom came up to me and gave me a kiss on the cheek. "Anything develops with this professor's murder, you keep me up-to-date, all right, darling?"

CHAPTER 7

I GO TO WORK at nine in the morn-
ing, but I'm never up before eight-fifteen. A quick
shower, a mouthful of orange juice, then I'm in my car,
on my way. I prefer my sleep to my breakfast.

The morning after the murder I tiptoed through my
waking-up routine, not wanting to disturb Mom. I was
sure she'd be sleeping till noon at least, after the strenuous day she'd just had. But when I got downstairs, I
found she was up already, and a delicious salami-and-egg
smell greeted me from the kitchen.

"Mom, it's really nice of you," I said, "but I never eat
breakfast. I don't have time."

"You've got time to ruin your stomach?" she said. "Sit
down, eat. There's nobody in the world that can't spare
five minutes. Even the president of the United States
eats a healthy breakfast."

I went into the kitchen and saw for the first time that
Mom had a guest, a large fat woman in her fifties whose
good-humored porklike face looked familiar to me.

38

Mom introduced her as Mrs. Cassidy, and it turned out she lived in a house two doors down.

"Julie is driving me to the supermarket in a few minutes," Mom said. "You got nothing in your icebox, did you know that?"

"Mom, the icebox is full."

"Nothing that a healthy person can eat. It's very nice of you, Julie."

"Think nothing of it," said Mrs. Cassidy, with a hearty laugh that had a lot of chest behind it. "You can tell me more about your life as a little girl on the Lower East Side. It's fascinating."

"Can you believe it, Julie was never in New York?" Mom said. "She was born in this state, and got married here to a man that worked for the electric company, and now she's a widow she hates the idea of traveling alone. I'm telling her, she should come East and visit me sometime, I'll put her up in the spare room and show her all the sights. Maybe we'll go out and enjoy the nightlife."

Mrs. Cassidy's laugh boomed out even louder. "This mother of yours, she's got more pizzazz than my daughter, and *she's* twenty-five!"

What I found most amazing was, I'd been living in this neighborhood for a year, seeing Mrs. Cassidy off and on every week, and I didn't even know her name. In less than a day, Mom knew her whole life history, and they were bosom buddies.

Satisfied that I was eating my breakfast, Mom stood up, ready for the expedition to the supermarket. I offered to give her some money for the groceries, but she said, "Foolishness. I'm living here, I'll pay my share."

She came up to me and hugged me, and then the ladies left. I heard them chugging off in Mrs. Cassidy's station wagon. I gulped some coffee—Mom did make terrific coffee—and went chugging off, too.

My office is downtown, in the courthouse, a block-long building designed in a kind of Greco-Pueblo style. It has Doric columns and a spacious portico, but these classic architectural features are painted pink to look like adobe. A small tower juts up from the middle of the roof, with an imitation mission bell in it.

This edifice was put up less than a year ago, two blocks away from the old courthouse, which was torn down to make way for an office complex. There was a lot of rhetoric at the time, from our mayor, several local judges, and the media, to the effect that our new courthouse would be a model for such structures all over the United States. The newspaper ran an editorial informing us that justice in Mesa Grande would finally be housed in a temple sufficiently magnificent and up-to-date to do it proper honor.

Our district attorney, Marvin McBride, then moved his staff and his offices into the plum areas of the new courthouse. Their rooms are twice as big as their rooms in the old building were; their carpets are twice as thick, and their air-conditioning twice as cold; and in consequence their egos have grown twice as large.

The public defender also moved into the new courthouse. Our offices—is it necessary for me to say?—aren't nearly as spacious and splendid as those of the district attorney. Ann Swenson has one small room on the top floor, at the back of the building; her secretary has an adjoining alcove; and I'm squeezed into another adjoining room, which I suspect was originally meant to be a broom closet.

I got to the courthouse before nine that morning, but even this early it was crowded. To tell you the truth, I enjoy it like that—noisy, bustling, full of thuggish-looking types rubbing elbows in the hallways with buttoned-down bespectacled young-lawyer types. And you can't always be sure which of these types are the lawyers and which the thugs.

At the newsstand in the courthouse lobby, I picked up

40

an early edition of our local paper. The Bellamy murder was a headline above the masthead, but only the sketchiest account of it was given. I took the elevator up to our office, and found Ann's secretary, Mabel Gibson, stationed in my doorway. "She wants to see you," Mabel said. "She just sent me to get you. I think it's about this awful murder. Oh, that poor young man! I understand his mother is still alive!"

Mabel is a sweet middle-aged lady, with a contented husband, grown and married children, a grandchild on the way, and an incurably sentimental view of life. God knows how she manages to hold on to it after all these years of working in the company of lawyers.

Ann was on the phone when I entered her office, and she waved at me to take a seat. And I thought, not for the first time, what a good-looking girl she was. Blond and willowy. You look at her, you think she couldn't have a brain in her head. The local graveyards are planted with prosecuting attorneys who made that mistake.

Occasionally I've asked myself why, if I admire her so much, something never got started between us. The first answer is, she's twenty years younger than me, I don't believe in cradle-snatching. The second answer is, she's such a smart woman, most likely she's smarter than I am—like Shirley was, as a matter of fact—and the truth is I couldn't handle that yet. But the third answer makes the first two irrelevant: Ann happens to have a perfectly good husband of her own, Joe Swenson, a local nose-and-throat specialist.

She got off the phone, and then she told me the news. Mike Russo had been arrested early this morning for Bellamy's murder. He had asked for Ann to defend him, giving as his reason not only that he didn't have much money but also that he had so much faith in me.

"You don't look particularly surprised at the news,"

Ann said. "You've got some reason to think we'll be defending a guilty client?"

"No. Certainly not. Only—" I told her about the look of hatred Mike had darted at Bellamy before the poetry reading, and what he had said to me afterward about being on the verge of committing a murder.

Ann's only reaction was "I hope nobody *heard* him saying that to you."

Before I could answer that, the buzzer sounded and Mabel Gibson was telling her, through the intercom, that Mr. Atwater had arrived.

Bill Atwater was a junior partner in the local law firm that handled legal business for Mesa Grande College. He was in his thirties, but dressed twenty years older than that, with a dark suit and a vest. Still fairly unusual attire for this section of the country, though the infiltration of yuppiedom is increasing every day.

He assured Ann that he wasn't here to assist us in our handling of Professor Russo's defense; he was here strictly as an observer for the college. He didn't look too happy about it, and I could understand why. The college's position was certainly tricky. Was it supposed to express sympathy for its poor dead professor, struck down in the course of duty? Or was it supposed to stand by its living professor, insisting on his right to be presumed innocent until proven guilty? Somehow it had to take both lines at the same time, and Atwater had the job of stage-managing this acrobatic feat. I didn't envy him.

"Well, what do you think?" he said to Ann. "They can't have much of a case, can they? It's just one of the district attorney's usual political maneuvers, isn't it? Getting mileage out of local hostility toward the college. I mean, college professors simply don't go around killing one another!"

"You're probably right," Ann said. "They take their aggressions out on their students—at least, that's how it

42

was when *I* went to college. On the other hand, the DA must have *something*. He's called a press conference for ten. He wouldn't be letting himself in for the publicity if he thought he was going to look like a damned fool."

"What *can* he have? Have you got any idea?"

"I will pretty soon. In two minutes I've got an appointment with the assistant DA who's handling the case. After that, I'll go over to the jail and talk to our client."

"And get him out on bail, I suppose?" I said.

"If I can. I don't know yet what position the assistant DA will be taking on that."

"Who's the assistant DA?"

"Well, we've had a bad break there. They've assigned George Wolkowicz to the case."

I knew what she meant. Wolkowicz was an ambitious young barracuda who clearly had plans to move on from Mesa Grande as soon as possible. He was marking time here, prosecuting the small-fry criminals until he could grab his chance to hobnob with the big-shot criminals in some first-class city.

Ann looked at her watch, then got to her feet. "Time for my meeting. You come with us if you want, Bill. It's important for us not to be late. Let's not give our esteemed district attorney and his hatchet man any excuse to enjoy their favorite dish—my scalp."

43

CHAPTER
8

OUR MEETING WITH Assistant DA George Wolkowicz took place in room 211. This was an ominous sign of how the district attorney's office felt about this case.

Room 211 is a small office—nothing in it but a desk and a few hard chairs—where the district attorney or one of his deputies sometimes meets with prisoners, their lawyers, and their relatives. It's located far away from the spacious, elaborately decorated suite of offices in which these august officials give interviews to the press, entertain community bigwigs, or do business with important allies and adversaries. Room 211 is reserved for people who, in the district attorney's opinion, are as good as dead.

Wolkowicz was sitting at the desk when we came in. He was a short, dark, wiry man in his early thirties, and belligerence radiated from him as it does from a lot of other small objects: Pekingese dogs, bumblebees, compact cars.

He gave a sharp nod at each of us, frowning a little

when he got to Atwater. "Why are you here, counselor? You know the public defender is prohibited by statute from bringing in any outside legal assistance, even if it's only for consultation purposes."

Atwater repeated his line about merely being an observer for the college.

This was enough to keep Wolkowicz from kicking him out of the room. The average citizen of Mesa Grande may resent "those rich college punks" and "those radical professors," but among the people who really count in our town, the people with the money and the power, there are many who went to the college or sent their children there or contribute to it generously. Of the consortium of five millionaires who own The Richelieu hotel, for instance, two of them are on the college's Board of Trustees.

"Oh sure, the college." Wolkowicz managed to make "college" sound like a dirty word. He himself had been a scholarship student at a big state university. "Well, no reason why you shouldn't sit in on this, if it's okay with Ann. This office is happy to cooperate with the college. We'd love to save it from embarrassment—though you have to admit, that might be a little tough in this case, since it's one of your professors who got killed and another one who killed him. The college pretty much seems to be involved at both ends, doesn't it?"

Wolkowicz gave a little laugh, then he put on his hard-hitting assistant-DA manner. "Okay, lady and gentlemen, I'm going to level with you. If the reason you asked for this meeting is you want us to set bail for Russo, you're wasting your time. This office is going to recommend he stay behind bars until the trial. No bail."

"Is that your personal decision, George," Ann asked, "or have you cleared it with Marvin?"

Wolkowicz reddened slightly. He never liked the suggestion that he had to clear things with Marvin McBride.

"That's my decision," he said. "I've got full responsibility for this case, Marvin's tied up today."

He didn't have to go into details. We all knew what District Attorney Marvin McBride was tied up with. The courthouse wits dub him "Sauce" McBride; according to legend, the reason why he tries so few cases personally is that trials have a way of beginning first thing in the morning and McBride never has his hangover under control before noon.

"Why are you taking such a tough line on this?" Ann said. "You're not dealing with a hardened criminal. Mike Russo is a college professor, his job and his ties are here in Mesa Grande, he hasn't got any criminal record. There's absolutely no indication he'd be likely to jump bail."

"It's a matter of policy. We always oppose bail when the death penalty could be involved."

"The death penalty! George, you must be kidding. Your office hardly ever asks for the death penalty."

"That all depends on how strong a case we've got, doesn't it? If it looks like we can't miss getting a conviction on the evidence—"

"What evidence? The early edition of the paper didn't even mention that Mike Russo's been arrested."

"That's right, we won't be giving out the story of his arrest till Marvin's press conference in half an hour or so. We wanted to be sure of our ground."

He gave a little grin, quietly nasty. "I don't know if the district attorney would approve of my laying out our whole case for you, but since you'll be reading all about it for yourselves in the paper— We'll begin with motive, okay? We can establish without a doubt that your client had a lot to gain from Stuart Bellamy's death."

"What did he have to gain?"

"You know anything about the system of tenure they've got at Mesa Grande College?"

Ann told him she did. It's the same system they have

46

at most colleges. When young teachers get hired after they've received their doctorate, they're on probation for six years. Then, if the college wants to keep them on, they get tenure—which means, if they don't actually bomb one of the buildings or rape a student, they've got the job for life.

"What you may not know," Wolkowicz said, "is that Russo and Bellamy were both hired at the same time, six years ago, to teach American literature. There were two tenure-track jobs then, and both of them could've been kept on. But a few months ago, on account of the economy and decreasing enrollments in the English department, the college decided it would have to get along with only one of them. The department had a meeting about it over the weekend, and they voted to recommend Bellamy for the job."

"And Mike Russo knew about this decision?" Ann said.

"Damned right he did. The chairman of the department—his name is Marcus Van Horn—told him about it a couple of days ago. What's more, he told him it was a close decision, that everybody wanted him, only they just happened to want Bellamy more. In other words, he implied that your client would get the job if Bellamy couldn't take it."

"But surely," said Atwater, "you're not contending that a man would commit murder simply in order to get hold of—of a professorship?"

What was going through his mind, of course, was that his starting salary in his law firm had been higher than most college professors were making after twenty years.

"It's a matter of perspective, isn't it?" Wolkowicz said. "How badly did he want the job? What would be his chances, if he got fired, of getting another one? Van Horn says the job market for college professors is pretty tight nowadays—especially in the field of English. Somebody who doesn't get tenure, he says, might easily be forced to give up teaching altogether."

Ann said, "Whether or not that's a convincing motive, George, is what we'll argue in court, isn't it? Offhand I'd say you'd better have a lot more on our client than that, if you expect to get a jury to believe you."

"How about opportunity?" Wolkowicz said. "We know exactly, to the minute, when the victim was killed. He was talking over the phone at five minutes to eight when the murderer attacked him. Several people heard him talking and noticed the time when he was cut off. You heard him yourself, didn't you, Dave? And noticed the time?"

I had to admit I did.

"Russo was supposed to be at the Van Horn party at that same time," Wolkowicz went on, "but he didn't show up. He didn't get there till after nine. He says he overslept, but he can't come up with any corroboration for that."

"Since he doesn't claim he was sleeping *with* somebody," Ann said, "I don't see how you can expect him to produce a witness."

"Oh, sure. But the fact remains, he can't prove where he was at the time of the murder."

"Bellamy probably had a dozen other acquaintances who can't prove where they were either."

"Maybe so. But how many of them can we definitely place at the scene of the crime?"

Wolkowicz let us stare at him for a moment, enjoying the effect he was making. Then he went on, "Luckily for us, the ground is still wet out in that neighborhood. The police did some looking around, and they found the impressions of a car that was parked by the curb half a block away from Bellamy's house. A funny place to park, because there's no house there, just a vacant lot. Almost like somebody didn't want any passersby to notice his car in front of the Bellamy house."

"And you're saying this parked car was Russo's?"

"The police made plaster casts of the tire tracks, and also of the tires on your client's car—it's a 1981 Dodge two-door. There's no doubt about it, it's the same car."

"The ground's been wet for almost a week," Ann said. "Russo may have parked his car near Bellamy's house days ago. He probably went to visit him over the weekend—"

"It's a theory," Wolkowicz said. "The trouble is, Russo tells us he *didn't* visit Bellamy over the weekend. What's more, his front left tire got a blowout yesterday morning, and he bought a new one and had it put on late yesterday afternoon. And sure enough, the front left tire mark near Bellamy's house matches up perfectly with Russo's new tire. Sorry, but you can't get around it. Your client was out there last night—and we all know what he was doing there, don't we?"

He settled back in his chair, and nobody said anything for a while.

Then Ann said, "What about the time of death? Does it square with the phone conversation?"

"As close as it has to," Wolkowicz said. "The medical examiner did a preliminary examination last night. Pending the autopsy, he says the deceased died from massive hemorrhaging, fracture, and concussion. He might've died instantaneously, or it might have taken him a while, head wounds being notoriously tricky. But in any case, he hadn't been dead more than an hour when he was found."

"And the paperweight definitely killed him?"

"Absolutely. The lab finished with it early this morning."

"Did it have any fingerprints on it?"

"A couple of smudges—somebody tried to wipe it off and didn't do a perfect job of it."

"But good enough so the smudges can't be identified?"

49

"A few years ago that might've been true," Wolkowicz said. "But there's this new technique now for bringing out fingerprints that used to be impossible to identify. There's a lab in Denver that does that sort of thing, the paperweight is on its way there right now. Not that it matters all that much. In our opinion, our case against your client is strong enough even if it turns out there are no fingerprints."

He rose suddenly to his feet, grinning more nastily than ever. "I've got another appointment. We'll have to cut this short. I'll end up the way I began, okay? No bail."

"Isn't that up to the judge, George?" Ann said. "Won't that be decided at the hearing this afternoon? Or doesn't the district attorney's office bother with the formality of going to court anymore?"

She flashed him *her* nastiest grin, and swept out of room 211, with Atwater and me right behind her.

CHAPTER 9

THE NEXT STOP FOR Ann and me was the jail, so that we could have a talk with Mike Russo. Atwater excused himself, though, saying he had a lot of work to do back at the college. He walked away from us quickly, and with great relief, I guessed. He and his three-piece suit felt slightly unclean after an hour of slumming.

Ann and I made our way along the underground corridor, dimly lit and smelling damp and musty, which connects the courthouse with the county jail. There we had to wait for half an hour, and then we were ushered into the crummy little room where prisoners confer with their lawyers. It has a wooden table in the center with two chairs on either side of it, and there's only one door, a heavy iron door with a small barred window set into it. A uniformed policeman stands outside this window throughout the interview, showing the world that he has a gun in a holster at his hip.

A few minutes later Mike was brought into the room by a guard. He was shaved, his hair was no more unruly than usual, and his clothes weren't particularly rumpled, but on his face was the look of a man who'd been through the wringer. He was wearing handcuffs. One of the things I've never been able to get used to is people wearing handcuffs.

The guard took Mike's off him and left the room. Mike stared down at his wrists, as if he was seeing them for the first time.

Then he gave a quick shake of his head and looked up at me. "Dave—I don't know how to thank you. I asked for you, but I couldn't be sure—" He turned to Ann. "It's good of you to come, Mrs. Swenson."

Ann gave one of her grunts. "Don't thank me, it's my job. When a prisoner wants the public defender, all he has to do is ask."

"Does that mean—you *will* take my case?"

"I don't have any choice in the matter, unless my caseload is too heavy at the time you ask me. Then I can dig up another lawyer for you, and the court'll appoint him. But my caseload is light enough just now. You don't get all that many major crimes in this cold weather. The second-story men and the muggers are mostly down in Florida working on their suntans."

"Well, I'm grateful, I want you to know."

"Fine. Now let's get to work. You sit there." She motioned Mike to the chair facing hers, across the wooden table, and I sat off to the side.

"Before I ask you any questions," Ann said, "one thing has to be clear between us. I'm your attorney. Everything you tell me is confidential. I'm not permitted to repeat it to anybody else, without your permission— that's the law. And that goes for Dave, too, as my representative. So what that means is, you can tell me the truth."

"Of course I'll tell you the truth."

"Why of course? Most of my clients lie to me, one time or another. Even if they're not guilty, they get the

52

crazy idea it'll be better for them if they lie to me. It *is* a crazy idea, that's what I want you to understand. Lying to your lawyer is the best way to get your balls turned into hamburger, you follow me?"

Mike was getting a little pale. Looking scared, which was exactly the state of mind Ann wanted him in. "I won't— I'll try not to lie to you," he said.

"Good. Now I'll ask you some questions." Ann leaned forward in her chair and fixed a steady gaze on him. "Did you kill him?"

Mike's words came out softly, while he looked down at his lap. "No, I didn't do it."

"Who are you saying that to?"

"Why, I'm saying it to you—"

"Then look at me when you talk to me. Are you afraid to look me in the face?"

"No, I'm not!" Mike's voice flashed with anger as he lifted his eyes and met Ann's gaze. "I didn't kill anybody—is that clear enough?"

Ann leaned back, poker-faced. "Clear enough. Now tell me everything you did last night, from the time you got home from work to the time you finally showed up at Marcus Van Horn's party."

"Well, my last class was over around three, and I drove home—no, wait a minute, I didn't drive home, because I didn't have my car. It blew a tire yesterday morning while I was on my way to school, and I didn't have a spare, so I had to call the AAA and get them to tow me to the Firestone repair center. And after class, I walked downtown and picked up the car with the new tire on it."

"Which wheel was it on?"

"The—uh—front left."

"So once you collected your car, you drove straight home?"

"Right. It was a little before four when I got there."

"And you live alone? You're not married?"

"Not yet, thank God."

"All right, you're in the house. Then what?"

"I worked for an hour or so, correcting student papers. That's always pretty depressing, so around five I put some music on the stereo and started fixing my dinner. That's a little early for me, but I was supposed to meet Dave at Marcus Van Horn's house at seven-thirty—"

"What music did you put on the stereo?"

"Let me see—Bartok. The Sonata for Two Pianos and Percussion. It's kind of loud and dissonant."

"Do you think any of your neighbors heard it?"

"I doubt it. I like it to blast out at me, and the neighbors used to complain, but since then I've been shutting the doors and windows whenever I turn on the stereo. They haven't complained lately, so I assume that's been doing the trick."

"While the music was on you fixed your dinner?"

"That's right. You want to know what I had? Spaghetti and meat sauce, courtesy of Chef Boyardee. Followed by mint-chip ice cream. The whole thing washed down with a bottle of beer. Coors Light, if that'll help you any. And after dinner I went to sleep."

"That was around what time?"

"Six thirty-five on the dot. I looked at the clock, because I set the alarm for seven. I don't live too far from Van Horn's house, takes me ten minutes to get there, but I had to put on my good suit before I left. Our chairman is always saying how informal his parties are, everybody should relax and let their hair down. But the fact is, if you show up without a jacket and a tie he gives you a very unfriendly look."

"So you never expected to get more than twenty-five minutes' sleep?"

"That's right."

"Doesn't seem worth the bother of lying down, not to mention taking the chance of oversleeping."

"I know that. To tell you the truth, I don't really understand what came over me. I wasn't even particularly tired when I got home yesterday. But I was just finishing dinner when this sudden drowsiness hit me. My head was whirling, and I could barely keep my eyes open. I told myself I couldn't show up at Van Horn's and fall asleep in his living room, so I decided to take a quick nap.

"The next thing I knew it was after eight-thirty. My alarm was still ringing, it must've been ringing since seven, that's what finally woke me up. I had one hell of a headache, but I rushed like hell to get some clothes on and put my hair in more or less reasonable shape, and I drove like a maniac. I got to Marcus' house a little after nine—and a few minutes later the law showed up."

"They didn't arrest you then, though."

"They asked me a lot of questions, and around eleven-thirty or so they let me go. It never occurred to me they weren't satisfied—it never occurred to me that *anybody* could think— Well, they were on my doorstep bright and early this morning, and now you know as much as I do."

He kept his eyes anxiously on Ann's face. As usual, though, there was nothing anybody could read there. The Great Deadpan, that was Ann Swenson when she was talking to a witness, and a lot of the time when she wasn't.

"Okay," Ann went on, "you know there's evidence your car was parked near Bellamy's house last night— and *after* you got your new tire?"

"Yes, the assistant DA's been asking me about that all morning. I just can't understand how my car got out to Stu Bellamy's neighborhood. I didn't drive out there yesterday, before or after I got my new tire."

"Could somebody else have driven your car out to Bellamy's house, maybe during that hour and a half you were sleeping?"

"I've wondered about that. But I'm damned if I can see how. There's only the one set of keys. Obviously I

55

had them with me when I drove home yesterday afternoon, and I had them with me later when I drove to Van Horn's house."

"Have you ever lost them?"

"No, I can't— Wait a second, here's a funny thing. A couple of days ago I was having lunch at the college cafeteria when I happened to notice my key ring was missing. It has all my keys on it—to the house, to my office, and the car keys. I didn't have any idea where I might've left it—I'd been in two different classrooms that morning, and had a conference with my chairman in his office, and dropped in to see a couple of my colleagues. But when I got back to my office after lunch, there was the key ring, sitting right on my desk. I didn't remember taking it out while I was in there earlier, but that must've been what I did."

"Tell me some more about your dinner," Ann said. "How did the food taste to you?"

"Same as usual. I didn't notice anything—"

"Was there anything you ate last night that you're *always* in the habit of eating? Some favorite food that everybody knows you like?"

"Well, I guess everybody knows how crazy I am about mint-chip ice cream. It's kind of a joke, the way I always order it when I go out. Come to think of it, there's another funny thing."

"What?"

"I didn't even realize, when I started fixing my dinner last night, that I *had* any mint-chip ice cream. I thought I'd run out of it, and nothing was left but chocolate and strawberry. Only, when I looked in the icebox, it turned out to be just the opposite. There was no chocolate or strawberry, nothing there but this carton of mint chip."

"A new unopened carton?"

"No, it was opened, about half full."

"Do you still have that carton in your refrigerator?"

"Well, no. Actually I ate all of it—there wasn't really that much—so I threw the carton away."

Ann sighed. "I don't suppose you know of anybody who might confirm your story about last night? Nobody called you on the phone while you were in your house? Nobody came to the door?"

"If anybody came to the door, I didn't open it for them. I was dead to the world. And I've got one of those phones where you can turn the noise level down to practically nothing. I did that when I started my nap."

"What about your car? At nine o'clock, when you drove it from your house to Van Horn's, did you notice anything out of the ordinary?"

"It drove the same as usual. I always have a little trouble getting it started, it's kind of old—"

"It's fifteen miles or so from your house to Blackhawk Road. Did you notice if your mileage had gone up thirty miles from when you drove home yesterday afternoon? Or if there was less gas in the tank than you would've expected?"

"I never pay attention to things like that. I'm sorry, I'm just not the kind of person who treats his car as if it were his baby."

"You know Bellamy was on the phone, talking to people at Van Horn's party, when he got killed?"

"Yes, I've heard."

"You were there, I understand, when Bellamy and Samantha Fletcher had the conversation that led to that phone call?"

"Sure, the great Richard Wright controversy. It was last week sometime. Stu and Samantha and I were through with our office hours, we were in the lounge having a cup of coffee. And the usual argument along with it."

"What's the usual argument?"

"Oh, Samantha saying that in every society and every

57

period of history men have been afraid to accept women as equals. And Stu saying that, even if there's been prejudice and discrimination in most if not all societies, there's always been a reaction against it, too. The really great writers and philosophers and so on have always championed human rights and equality of the sexes.

"Well, the upshot of it this time was, Samantha challenged Stu to mention a single male writer who wasn't a sexist. And Stu, not being the type to sit still for a direct challenge, came up with Richard Wright—he's a black writer who wrote in the forties and fifties. Stu said there were passages in Wright's autobiography *Black Boy,* and particularly the very last paragraph, that completely contradicted her wholesale condemnation of male writers. Samantha told him to show us that paragraph, and she guaranteed that what it would really prove was that Wright's concern was for black men, that he was fundamentally indifferent to the rights of black women.

"So Stu said he'd dig up the paragraph when he got home—he knows, knew, more about American black writers than anybody else on the faculty, including any of the blacks. But neither of us got a call from Stu that night, so I figured we wouldn't be hearing any more on the subject."

"Why did you think so?"

"I figured he'd looked up the paragraph in *Black Boy* and found out Samantha was right about it, so he was going to let it drop. To tell you the truth, I couldn't have been more surprised when I heard he phoned Samantha at that party to read her the passage. I mean, it proved that *she* was right and *he* was wrong, and Stu just wasn't the type who enjoys admitting when he's wrong."

Ann nodded and then, without raising her voice or changing her expression or giving any indication that she was about to pounce on him like a tiger out of the underbrush, she said, "What did you mean by what you told

Dave at the poetry reading the night before last—that you were on the verge of committing a murder?"

Mike darted me a look, kind of reproachful. I met it with no expression at all.

He turned back to Ann. "That was a damn fool thing to say, I know it. I was out of my mind—I'd just heard about this tenure business—"

"What about this tenure business?" Ann said. "You wanted tenure, and you knew you'd get it if Bellamy was out of the way. Didn't that make you feel like killing him?"

Mike couldn't have been paler. But he didn't lower his eyes again. He kept them on Ann's face. "I'm not supposed to lie to my lawyer? All right, I'll tell you exactly how I felt. Marcus Van Horn called me into his office on Tuesday afternoon, that was the day of the poetry reading, and broke the news to me, and—God, I hate that office of his!"

"Why so?"

"You've never been in it, I suppose. Nobody knows how many years it's been since he saw the top of his desk. It's a foot thick with old memos which he's probably never read, student papers which he might someday get around to correcting, manuscripts, newspaper clippings, a tape-recording machine with tapes scattered all around it, open books, a torn poster from the Old Vic, 1957. Somewhere under all that debris is his office telephone, but half the time, when it rings, he can't find it in time to answer. And most of this junk is overflowing onto the floor, you can't move six inches without tripping over something. Looks like a bombed city—very appropriate place for a death sentence!"

"If you lost your job at the college," Ann said, "would it really be a death sentence for you?"

Mike managed to keep his voice steady. "Suppose I give you a little bit of autobiography—is that all right? I

59

was born in the east Bronx. Do you know that section at all? You must know it, Dave, you're from New York. Mostly Italians in those days, the blacks and Puerto Ricans have driven them out in the last few years. When my father died I was in junior high school, and he didn't have much to leave to my mother and me. Nothing but the store—he sold and repaired phonographs and TV sets—but we couldn't get rid of it because the bills and debts were more than it was worth. So Mom took it over, and kept it going, God knows how."

"You couldn't give her much help?"

"I worked in the store on weekends and in the summer, but never on school days. She wouldn't let me. Nothing was going to interfere with school. She knew how things worked in America, how you don't get ahead unless you've had an education. She rode herd on me every night, making me do my homework and get good grades. She didn't let me get distracted by girls and parties. I got a full scholarship to Stanford, and later to grad school at Yale, and I never would've done it if it wasn't for her."

"Did she always want you to become a college professor?"

"When I told her that's what I wanted to do, she gave me a look, as if her little boy had suddenly gone out of his mind. But I explained what it meant to me, how I wanted to teach the books I loved to people who were young enough so maybe I could make them love those books, too. She saw I was serious about it, and she stood behind me on it, whatever she might think about it herself."

"Your mother is still alive?"

"Yes, she's in this retirement home in Washington Heights. I go East to visit her on my vacations. Sometimes she gets confused, doesn't recognize me. But most of the time she's very alert, she spends her days bragging to her friends about her college professor son."

For a while he couldn't go on talking, then he said, "All right, I was jealous of Stu. I was angry and frustrated. I knew damn well why Van Horn and the rest of them were giving the job to him instead of to me. Because he was a member of the club. That nice cozy little WASP, prep-school, Ivy League, true-blue American majority club they all belong to. Talk about irony, for God's sake! I belong to a minority, so I don't get the goodies the majority reserves for itself. But I belong to the *wrong* minority—I'm not a black or a Chicano or a woman—so I don't get the leftovers the majority's willing to toss away. It's a crazy world we live in.

"All right, I admit it. Last night when I heard Stu was dead— Do you want me to pretend I was brokenhearted? The hell I was! *I'd* be getting tenure, and *he* got the death sentence! Excuse me—unless I get the death sentence, too."

His voice shook a little, then he got it under control. "But what happened to him—I never wished for *that*. I didn't kill him. I know you won't believe me—what I said to Dave, I know how bad it looks—but I swear to God I didn't kill him!"

Ann watched him a moment in silence, then got to her feet. "Okay, that's all for now. I'll see you at two this afternoon, you'll be getting a hearing on your request for bail."

"Do you think— Will they let me out on bail?"

"Who knows? Depends if you get a sympathetic judge."

"I hope so," he said. "Because you know—it really isn't so great in here."

He tried a smile, but it didn't work too well. The pain on his face looked genuine. If only you could tell the truth about people from looking at their faces.

CHAPTER 10

AS ANN AND I emerged into the street, I blinked my eyes and took a gulp of fresh air. I am not crazy about prisons.

I asked Ann if she'd be needing me at the bail hearing this afternoon, and she said she wouldn't. So we separated in front of the jail.

She had a lot of paperwork to do in connection with the case. That's one of the by-products of murder: It creates paperwork the way rabbits create rabbits. And I had a lot of legwork to do. Talk to Marcus Van Horn and Samantha Fletcher about that phone conversation. Talk to people who lived near Bellamy on Blackhawk Road, in case one of them heard or saw anything. Nose around the college and find out if Bellamy had any other enemies besides Mike Russo, if there was anybody else who might have a motive for killing him.

Before I got to any of these things, though, I had a date to have lunch with Mom. We had arranged this at breakfast this morning—I would meet her at noon at Tokyo Rosie's, a new Japanese restaurant a few blocks up from the courthouse. It was in the same location as the French place before it and the Italian place before that. There's always a big turnover in restaurants in Mesa Grande.

It was ten minutes before noon, so I picked up the late edition of the *Republican-American,* went to my table in the restaurant, and ordered a cup of coffee. While I sipped it—and incidentally, it was pretty vile: Oh well, the Japanese aren't supposed to be able to make coffee—I read the latest on the murder. A lot more detail this time, and Mike Russo, with pictures, was all over the front page.

The *Republican-American*—if you're looking for understatements—is a conservative newspaper. In the 1972 presidential election, it advised its readers not to vote, because McGovern and Nixon were both too far to the left. It did support Ronald Reagan in 1980, but it's been very upset with him lately. He's in the White House for six years, and kids still can't say prayers in the public schools. The editors haven't actually called him a Communist, but they're raising doubts about some of his advisers.

In covering the Bellamy murder, this sheet maintained its usual standard of journalistic accuracy and objectivity. This was the headline:

BLOOD BATH AT MESA GRANDE COLLEGE;
PROF KILLS PROF, SAYS DA MCBRIDE

From what followed a visitor from Mars would have learned that college professors as a class were slobbering psychopaths who continually went around murdering one another.

The paper also ran an interview with District Attorney Marvin McBride, in which he assured the citizens of Mesa Grande that the forces of justice had no intention of allowing these elitist so-called intellectuals to act as if they were above the law in *this* town.

I pushed this garbage aside, and thought for a while about that supreme proof of human irrationality, the success in our town of Marvin McBride.

To a lot of people around here it seems as if he's been our district attorney forever. Every four years he goes before the voters, with his pugnacious jaw and red-veined little face, and gets himself handily reelected. And immediately settles down to another four years of the sloppy, inefficient administration that characterized his office during all his previous terms. What's more, his high pluralities never suffer from the fact that everybody in town knows he's a hopeless lush.

He brings off this periodic miracle by knowing the way to the heart and mind of the ordinary Mesa Grande citizen. He knows that this is a town in which fundamentalist ministers have daily television shows; in which every third car has a "Honk for Jesus" bumper sticker; in which the only newspaper is somewhat to the right of Generalissimo Franco; in which there's one bookstore and no art movie house but at least a hundred stores that sell guns. McBride's campaign strategy consists entirely of hinting broadly, as often as possible, that if he isn't reelected, law and order will come to a stop and the bums, the Mafia, the college radicals, and the secular humanists will take over the city, burn the houses, rape the women, and turn our children into dope fiends and homosexuals.

Mom appeared in the doorway of the restaurant, waving at me, then came bustling over and took a seat. For a few seconds she caught her breath, then she looked around the restaurant. "In New York, when it's Japanese, you have to take off your shoes and sit on the floor. That's why I never go to them. Sitting on the floor is possible maybe, but at my age the problem is getting up again."

"I guess we just aren't as sophisticated as New York," I said. "We still like to sit down on chairs to eat our meals."

The waitress, a Japanese woman in a kimono, brought us our menus, and Mom frowned over the selection for a while. When I told her that sushi was mostly raw fish, she made a face and said, "The way I was brought up, we cooked our fish. The parts we didn't cook we fed to the cats."

She put in an order for yakitori and hot tea, and then settled down to telling me about her morning. Mrs. Cassidy had taken her to the supermarket, and Mom had been pleasantly surprised to find that most of the products she bought in New York supermarkets were also available here. "Who'd ever expect," she said, "that they'd have Campbell's soup all the way up in the mountains!"

I said that it was brought in every month by mule train, and she told me I had a fresh tongue in my head, but actually she wasn't the least bit annoyed, she was pleased at how her morning had gone and full of interest in the details of Mesa Grande life to which she'd been exposed.

"Believe it or not, they also had matzos and gefilte fish at the supermarket. I found them in the gourmet foods section."

After she got back from her grocery shopping and filled up my icebox with "decent things to eat," Mom had gone on a tour of the area with Mrs. Cassidy. But she didn't see any of the usual things that tourists are urged to see, the mountain views and spectacular red-rock formations. "Julie offered," Mom said, "but I told her rocks and mountains, you've seen one of them, you've seen them all. I told her what interested me was people. Every person is not only a little bit different from every other person but also exactly the same. So Julie took me to this organization she belongs to, where they've got activities for people who are retired or their families have moved out and they've got time on their hands."

"A senior citizens' club?"

"Senior citizens! Kindly don't use that expression to me. I'm a person, not a citizen. Citizens are for people that have to live in Russia. And why do you say 'senior' when what you mean is 'old'? So why not say it, 'old'? Is it a dirty word or something?"

"All right, Mom, Mrs. Cassidy took you to some kind of old people's club that she belongs to?"

"Well, I didn't see any teenagers there. The rock and roll wasn't coming out of the jukebox."

"They had a jukebox?"

"Naturally. You think, once you're over seventy, you lose your taste for music? Sometimes you can't hear it so good anymore, but I'm lucky that's no problem of mine. There was one room they were playing records in all the time I was there—old songs your father and I used to dance to when we were young." Mom shut her eyes and started humming and murmuring the words. " 'The birds do it, the bees do it—' Now those were songs. Nice sexy words to them, and you could understand what was being sung. Today everybody's yelling, but who can figure out what the words are? It's like this younger generation is afraid of sex. You think maybe that's why the population isn't exploding anymore?"

"You never used to like old people's clubs, Mom. You told me a few years ago you'd rather spend a social evening in a leper colony."

Mom shrugged. "Different circumstances, different feelings, am I right? The places I don't like are in New York, they're full of old *kockers* can't do anything except tell you about their aches and pains and how their children don't come to visit them enough. Here in this town of yours people don't talk so much, maybe it's because they're Westerners, they don't have as much inside their heads as New York people, but for a change it's restful. Julie introduced me to a couple friends of hers, nice people, both sexes, and we carried on a civilized conversation without being interrupted every two minutes by somebody's arthritis."

The waitress brought our food, and then Mom said very casually, "So I'm reading in the paper this morning, they arrested your friend the English professor for the murder last night, and the public defender is taking his case."

"That's right, Mom."

"So what's the details? Do you know what kind of evidence they've got against him?"

To talk to Mom about the case would be strictly unprofessional, as I knew perfectly well. Still, I didn't even go through the motions of an inner conflict. I started right in, telling her everything that had happened this morning.

"So what's your opinion?" she said, when I had finished. "Is your boss defending a guilty client?"

"A lawyer isn't supposed to consider such a question. Every defendant is innocent until proven guilty. Every accused person is entitled to the best legal defense he can get. That's the American—"

"All that I know," Mom said, brushing it away. "But even a lawyer is entitled to a personal opinion—and you're not even a lawyer. So what's your personal opinion?"

"I keep seesawing back and forth. Sometimes I think he's guilty as hell. I mean, he did have a motive, and a good strong one, though Ann'll do her damnedest to belittle it in court. It seems perfectly natural to me that a man nowadays would kill somebody to keep from losing his job."

"Especially if it's a job you can't get fired from," Mom said, nodding. "This tenure business—wonderful! Your

67

father should've had such a thing in cloaks and suits when he was a young fellow."

"And he can't account for himself when the murder was being committed," I went on. "That story about oversleeping—I can imagine what George Wolkowicz will do to him if he tells that in court. The fact is, nobody saw him for five hours or so. He had plenty of time to drive out to Bellamy's place, kill him at five to eight, drive back to his house, change his clothes if he happened to get any blood on them, and show up at the party a little after nine. And the clincher, of course, is that his car *was* parked down the street from Bellamy's house some time after four o'clock when the new tire was put on it. Motive, opportunity, and he's been placed at the scene of the crime. What else could anyone ask for, short of his committing the murder in front of a room full of people?"

"Which he practically did, in a way," Mom said. "But you say you're seesawing. What's the opposite side of the seesaw?"

"A couple of things. The line Ann is planning to take, obviously, is that somebody's framing Mike for the murder. Somebody who knows about his motive managed to steal his keys and get them duplicated, then slipped into his house and put some kind of knockout drops into his mint-chip ice cream, then drove his car out to Blackhawk Road, parked it where the tire marks were sure to be discovered, killed Bellamy, and brought the car back."

"And how do you feel about this idea?"

"Well, it does take care of one of the peculiarities you pointed out last night. Why did the murderer kill Bellamy while Bellamy was talking over the phone? Why take the chance that his victim might have time, before he lost consciousness, to blurt out his murderer's name to the party at the other end of the line?

"The answer is, if the murderer was trying to frame

Mike, then he—or she, I suppose—would *want* Bellamy to make that phone call. Because what would have happened if there *hadn't* been any phone call? The exact time of the murder wouldn't have been established, Mike wouldn't have stood out from the crowd as somebody who didn't have an alibi, a new snowstorm—which, as a matter of fact, it looks as if we're about to get—would have covered up the tire marks that put Mike at the scene of the crime. In other words, the whole frame-up against Mike depended on Bellamy getting killed while he was talking on the phone."

Mom was beaming at me. "That's good," she said. "You've still got a brain in your head, even with this mountain air."

I actually found myself blushing when she said these words. Like a little kid getting a compliment from a grown-up.

"One point about your reasoning, though," Mom went on. "Like you said, Bellamy *could* have called out the murderer's name over the phone. This is quite a risk for the murderer to run, only for the purpose of framing somebody. Can you explain that, I wonder?"

"Maybe this murderer really has it in for Mike, hates him *and* Bellamy."

"Possible," she said, and for a moment there was a puzzled frown on her face.

We were finished eating, so I paid the check and we went out to the street. "Let me drive you home, Mom," I said.

"You don't have to. I'm taking a walk, it's only a couple blocks, to the YMCA where I'm meeting Julie Cassidy. They've got a bridge tournament there this afternoon, the two of us are thinking maybe we'll be partners."

"The YMCA, Mom? You know what those letters stand for, don't you? The Young Men's Christian Association."

"So? Your point is, I'm not young, I'm not a man, I'm not a Christian? Julie says the YMCA don't care about any of those things. She's not young or a man either, and she's always been a lousy Christian. All they care is, can you play bridge? So tell me, darling, what's your next step? What are you planning to do this afternoon?"

"I thought I'd go out to Blackhawk Road and talk to some of Bellamy's neighbors. Maybe somebody noticed something—another car parked in front of the house, a visitor—"

"Can I make a suggestion for something else you could do if you go out there?"

"Any suggestion is welcome, Mom."

"Go inside this Bellamy's house. Give it a good looking over. Especially the room where the murder happened. And especially the telephone."

"If there'd been any evidence in that room, Mom—if there was anything wrong with the phone—I'm sure the police would've found it. They're pretty efficient."

"You should never be so sure about how efficient people are. I had a cleaning woman for twenty years, every Thursday she came in, I swore by her. Last year she retired on account of water on her knee, and I got a new cleaning woman, and you know what was the first thing she found out? In all those years my old cleaning woman never once ran a rag along the back of the toilet cabinet, where it was a half-inch away from the wall. What we found on the back of that toilet cabinet! If this Japanese chicken you've got me eating wasn't so delicious, I'd be sick to my stomach remembering it."

"All right, Mom," I said, and couldn't keep from smiling, "I'll go inside that house and give it as much of a search as I can. Especially the phone—and the toilet cabinet."

"Thank you for humoring an old lady," she said.

She gave me a peck on the cheek, and I watched her marching down the street until she disappeared around the corner.

CHAPTER 11

FOR THE SECOND TIME in two days, I found myself heading out to Blackhawk Road.

In the sunlight, Bellamy's house looked like a bright gleaming freshly painted oasis in a desert of drab. I parked in front of it, and a uniformed patrolman, gray haired, close to retirement, came down the walk to meet me. He was starting to order me out of there, but as soon as I told him I was an investigator for the public defender, he offered to accompany me inside. The public defender—in theory, at any rate—is supposed to have the same access to evidence as the district attorney. Convictions have been overturned on appeal when it was proved that free access had been denied.

I entered the large hallway and peered around at the Oriental rug, the tall fat Chinese vase, the antique table it was standing on. What was I looking for? God knows. Mom had told me to give the place a "looking over," and mine but to do or die.

I stepped through the archway into the living room, the gray-haired cop right behind me. The murder scene looked a lot different than it had looked last night. It was a shambles, from the trampling of all those scientific specialists plus a herd of ordinary detectives who got a kick out of sticking their big clumsy hands into everything. One piece of clutter that was no longer there, of course, was the body, and the telephone had been returned to a small telephone table next to the desk.

"Mind if I take a look around?" I said to the policeman.

He shrugged. "Fine with me. You ain't going to find anything. They've been over this place a dozen times, anything that's evidence they already took away."

"Well, I have to do something to earn my salary," I said.

I started nosing around this room, with apparent aimlessness. Apparent? I *didn't* know what I was aiming at.

I ran my eyes over every inch of the floor, which was uncarpeted, a nice shiny finished wood. I got up on tiptoe and examined the tops of the bookcases, then continued the examination along every shelf. Remembering Mom's mysterious suggestion, I picked up the phone, peered at it closely, turned it upside down, took it off the hook and listened to the dial tone.

I came to the earth-shaking conclusion that it was a phone exactly like any other.

I got down on my knees to look at the piles of books on the floor. Mostly American stuff. Novels I'd read, and plenty more I'd never even heard of. A lot of it about blacks or by blacks.

I was getting up from my knees, when something attracted my attention. There was a space of about an inch or so between the bottom of the bookcase and the floor. In this space, way back where the wall and the floor came together, I caught a glimpse of something bright.

I didn't reach under the bookcase for it. I stood up and continued wandering around the room, but I wasn't actually looking at anything now, I was thinking hard.

I had a problem, no question about it. This bright object, whatever it was, had escaped the notice of the detectives who had searched the room. It might, it just might, have something to do with Bellamy's murder. Suppose it was something incriminating to Mike—a cufflink, say, or a key that could be identified as his. Then, obviously, it was my duty to slip it out from its hiding place and turn it over to Ann without the police knowing what I was doing.

On the other hand, suppose it was a piece of evidence indicating that somebody else might be the murderer. In that case, what I ought to do was keep my hands strictly away from it, call out to the uniformed cop that there was a shiny object under the bookcase, make sure that *he* reached for it and retrieved it. Otherwise, the DA would accuse me of having planted it there myself, and Ann wouldn't be able to use it in court.

But if I did *that,* and it turned out to be a piece of evidence that worked *against* Mike—

I tossed a mental coin and decided the lesser of two evils was to reach under the bookcase surreptitiously and bring the mysterious object out myself. After all, even if I had the cop bring it out, the DA would *still* accuse me of having planted it there. Since it probably wouldn't do us any good in court under any circumstances, I might as well take a look at it and decide where I wanted to go from there.

I said to the cop, "Who's at the front door?"

"I didn't hear the bell," he said.

"It wasn't the bell. A sort of rattling noise. As if somebody's trying the doorknob, trying to see if the house is unlocked."

"One of those damned neighborhood kids again! I'll be back in a jiffy!"

He went stamping out of the living room, and I was immediately on my knees again, reaching under the bookcase. I groped around until my fingertips came up against something sharp and metallic. I eased it toward me and was finally able to get a grip on it. I managed to

73

scoop it up, jump to my feet, and shove it into my over-coat pocket, just as the cop returned.

"Nobody there. They must've run off when they heard me coming."

"Probably my imagination," I said. "I've got this ten-dency to hear things."

"My mother-in-law had that problem for a while," he said. "They found out it was wax in her ears."

I told him I wanted to look through the rest of the house. So I returned to the hall and from there into the dining room and the kitchen, with the cop following me. Bellamy's refrigerator was full, and the shelves had a lot of canned goods on them: fancy stuff, potted shrimp and pâté and so on.

Then I went up the stairs to the second floor, the cop going up after me, of course. There were two large bed-rooms on the second floor, with a hallway between them, and a bathroom leading off the hallway. One bedroom had two life-size photographs on opposite walls: the head of William Faulkner and the head of Ernest Hemingway. They seemed to be glaring across the room at each other, as if they were about to step into the ring and fight it out for the World Championship. I assumed this had been Bellamy's own room.

"Did somebody make up the bed in here after the de-tectives got through searching?" I asked.

"Nobody did much of anything up here," he said. "They took a look upstairs, that's all. Far as I know, the bed wasn't touched."

I wandered around the room awhile, opened the dresser drawers and the drawers in the bed table, looked into the closet. Bellamy had an extensive wardrobe— you didn't buy that many clothes, and such high-priced ones, on an assistant professor's salary. But I didn't see anything anywhere that struck me as particularly out of the ordinary. For instance, I didn't see any photographs, framed or otherwise, that might hint at the existence of some woman, or even of some other human being, in Bellamy's life.

The second bedroom had even less to tell. It was obviously a guest room, it was neat as it could be, there were no sheets or pillowcases on the bed. Bellamy certainly hadn't had any guests there recently.

I moved out to the hall and went into the upstairs bathroom. The great discovery I made was that Bellamy had used after-shave lotion and underarm deodorant. Just for the hell of it, I ran my fingers along the back of the toilet bowl, where it was close to the wall. A little bit of dust, not much. Brilliant deduction—the cleaning woman hadn't been in for a couple of days.

I told the cop I was finished, thanked him for his cooperation, and left the house. The sky was purple, though there should still have been a few more hours of light.

What about the neighbors? I walked along the street and realized there were only two houses within a few blocks. All the people in them would've been questioned by the police already, of course, but I spent the next half hour ringing doorbells and questioning people again. I came up with absolutely nothing, which didn't surprise me a bit.

So I got into my car and started back to town. A snowflake fell on the windshield. Then several more. Before I'd gone another two blocks, the snow had reached the proportions of a flurry. That's how it goes in our section of the country. The local saying is "If you don't like the weather, stick around for an hour, it's bound to change."

A mile or so away from Bellamy's house, I pulled the car up to the curb and turned on the light. Then I reached into my pocket and took out the object I had retrieved from under Bellamy's bookcase. It was small and metal, with a piece of red glass set in it.

An earring.

CHAPTER 12

IT WAS AFTER TWO-THIRTY when I got back to the courthouse, hoping to show Ann what my search of Bellamy's house had produced. But she wasn't in, Mabel Gibson told me she was in court for Mike Russo's bail hearing and had no idea how long it would take.

"And look at the snow!" Mabel added. "I hope she goes straight home. I really worry about her driving her car in weather like this."

"I worry about you, too, Mabel," I said. "Why don't you go home before this gets too bad."

"Oh that's sweet of you, David, but I haven't got my car today, my husband is picking me up at five in our little truck. It's got four-wheel drive, so we're really quite safe."

I took the earring into my cubbyhole and studied it for a while. It was a cheap mass-produced item, nothing valuable about it at all. Was there anybody involved in this case who might be connected to it? Bellamy hadn't been wearing an earring, the one time I'd met him, and Mike

Russo didn't wear earrings either. Male college professors pretty much stayed away from such suspect adornments. What about Samantha Fletcher, had *she* been wearing earrings when I saw her at the poetry reading two nights ago or last night at Van Horn's party? No, I didn't think so.

At any rate, who could say how long this earring had been lying there under the bookshelf? Maybe somebody had lost it there months ago, long before the murder.

Except that the tidiness of the house suggested Bellamy had a cleaning woman who came in regularly. If the earring had been under his bookshelf for any length of time, how come the cleaning woman had never found it?

On the other hand, I remembered Mom's little lecture to me last night, about the efficiency of cleaning women.

I slipped the earring into my pocket and decided not to waste the afternoon waiting around for Ann. I drove up to the college, which was a sacrifice beyond the call of duty, because the snow was really heavy now and, if the truth were known, my windshield wipers had seen better days. The main problem with them was, they did a beautiful job of wiping the right-hand side of the windshield, but the left-hand side, where the driver sat, looked strictly like mush.

I got to my destination in one piece, though, and went to the college coffee shop. Nursing one cup of coffee and a doughnut, I sat at a booth in the corner and listened to what the students who sat near me were saying about the murder.

Mostly they seemed to be divided into two factions. One faction said that Mike Russo was guilty, and they thought he should get a medal for it—Bellamy had been asking to get himself killed for years. The other faction said that Mike was innocent: Some said it was because he was too nice a guy to kill anybody, he was positively not into violence; others said it was because he was your typical professorial wimp, too weak and indecisive to do anything as practical as commit a murder.

In addition to these factions, there were a number of individuals with highly imaginative theories. The president of the college killed Bellamy, because Bellamy was having an affair with his wife. (You should see his wife!) Bellamy was killed by a black activist who didn't approve of honkies teaching books by brothers. Bellamy was killed by a psycho who was going around the Southwest knocking off people who wear tweed jackets.

College students haven't changed much since my day, I thought. When time hangs heavy on their hands—in between drinking, fucking, and cracking the books—they enjoy spreading rumors.

I left the coffee shop and made my way, with the snow whipping my cheeks and clogging my nose, to Llewellyn Hall. It was nearly three-thirty, most of the faculty at Mesa Grande College ended their office hours around now—if they weren't of such scholarly eminence that they were absolved from holding office hours at all. If I didn't get up there pretty soon, there wouldn't be anybody around for me to talk to.

I went up to the second floor, where the English department was located, and found Marcus Van Horn's office. His voice rang out when I knocked, "Come in, come in!"

The office was total chaos, exactly the way Mike Russo had described it to me. The clutter was thickest in the area of the desk. There was nothing on that desk but books and papers, as far as I could tell, but they made it hard for me to see the occupant of the room; his head and shoulders seemed to be part of the debris. Only when he spoke—"Sit down, please take a seat!"—was I able to sort him out from the inanimate objects.

In order to accept his invitation, I had to remove several books from the chair. I couldn't see any clear surface to put them on, so I put them on the floor. Van Horn raised no objection.

I reminded him who I was and told him I was gathering information for Mike Russo's defense. Right away his face got very solemn, and he shook his head and made a little clucking sound with his tongue. "Terrible tragedy. Simply terrible. Poor Stuart! Poor Mike! Both such fine young men. Did you know, Mike is the sole support of his mother, who lives in some kind of old-age home in New York? Well, I'm certainly happy to give you any help I can. I should tell you, however, that you've come at a rather bad time. I usually leave my office around now, I'm engaged in a scholarly project, an interesting point about the relationship between Samuel Johnson's poetic style and the way he defines certain words in his dictionary. Late afternoon is when I do my research and dictate my notes."

"I'll try not to take up too much of your time," I said. "Could you tell me first about that phone call."

"Oh yes. Terrible, terrible. To actually *hear* a man being killed—well, you know what I mean, you heard it yourself, didn't you?"

"You're positive that *was* Professor Bellamy on the phone?"

"No doubt about it. His voice was unmistakable, that drawling tone of his. I've talked to him practically every working day for the last six years. I assure you, nobody could have imitated his voice with any chance of fooling me, if that's what you're wondering about."

"The call was for Professor Fletcher. How come you happened to get to the phone at the same time she did?"

"Well, let me see. I heard the phone ring, and naturally I wanted to answer it, but I was at the other end of the living room, and there was such a crush of people between me and the hallway. I always get quite a substantial crowd at these monthly gatherings of mine. What attracts people, I think, is the easy informality. Just a pleasant get-together, a totally nonthreatening atmosphere, at which my younger colleagues can rub elbows with some of us seasoned old veterans. The dean was there, and the president was invited, too, but of course he's out of town this week. He always manages to be out of town when some kind of campus crisis arises. The man's instincts are infallible—"

"So when you heard the phone ring, you started through the crowd to get to it?"

"Precisely. But by the time I got there, Samantha—Professor Fletcher—was already on the phone. You were there, too, as a matter of fact. I realized she was talking to Stu Bellamy—"

"Weren't you surprised to hear his voice?"

"How so?"

"According to what you told the police, he'd called you a few hours before to say he had a touch of the flu and wasn't feeling well enough to leave his house."

"Oh, yes, that's true. I did wonder if it was wise of him to use his voice under the circumstances. I wonder if that accounts for a certain oddness in his manner—or was I just imagining—?"

I leaned forward. "Imagining what?"

"The way he talked to Samantha, hardly acknowledging her greeting when she got on the phone, never addressing her by name. It was almost rude, and whatever anyone might say about Stu, nobody could ever accuse him of bad manners. He had the finest type of bringing-up. Such a fine family—Rhode Island people—the grandfather left him a nice bit of money, I believe."

"When you found out the reason for that phone call, did it surprise you?"

"No, not really. It arose, so I've been told, out of some dispute between Samantha and Stu—on some sort of feminist issue, of course."

"Why 'of course'?"

He smiled gently. "You've met Samantha, haven't you? She's our medievalist, the newest as well as the youngest member of our department. She's been with us only two or three years, a lovely young woman, and from what I hear an excellent teacher and a first-rate scholar. But after two minutes of conversation, she does let you know exactly what she is, doesn't she?"

He gave a little sigh. "I'm totally in sympathy with the principle of women's rights, you understand—equal pay for equal work, and so forth—but there's a certain fanaticism afoot these days, an urge to carry everything beyond the limits of common sense, not to mention good manners. Well, that's why the subject of her dispute with Stu Bellamy didn't surprise me."

"What about the book they were arguing about? Do you happen to be familiar with it?"

"Something by a black writer who was rather prominent in the forties, wasn't it? Now what was that title? *Black Beauty?*"

"*Black Boy.*"

"Oh, yes. I've never actually read the work, I'm afraid."

"How come?"

"Frankly, because life is too short. There are too many truly great masterworks I haven't read—and too many treasure troves to which I can return again and again, always finding new riches. After one reaches the age of sixty, one begins to hear Time's winged chariot drawing near. Why should I clutter my mind and use up my precious hours with second-rate stuff by second-rate people?"

"*Black Boy* is second-rate?"

"It's a topical work of some relevance to the racial tensions of our time, or so they tell me. And its sentiments are on the side of the angels, I'm sure. But after all, the racial tensions of our time will pass, won't they? And long after they fade away, the eternal verities, the universal issues the *greatest* writers concern themselves with will still be with us."

"Still, you didn't find it strange that an argument over a book should have been so important to Professor Bellamy? After all, he made that phone call even though he was in bed with the flu—"

"Good grief, that wasn't the least bit strange. In the world of academia, trivial disputes have a way of becoming important. That's the reason why poor Stuart's death, while it's certainly come to me as a shock, wasn't really a surprise."

"You expected somebody to kill him?"

"No, no, please don't misunderstand me. Not him specifically. All I'm saying is, the groves of academe aren't as serene and peaceful as the outside world would like to believe. Tensions, jealousies, ambitions, bitterness—all of these seethe beneath the surface of this ivory tower. And especially here at Mesa Grande, where we're isolated from the great world, no nearby centers of culture or intellectual life. We're forced in on ourselves, we're sardines in a can."

"You've been teaching here for nearly forty years, haven't you? How do you deal with these terrible tensions?"

"Through hobbies mostly. Recently I've become a total convert to the electronics age. I used to be something of a Luddite in my attitude toward machines. But since my dear Louise's passing, I've acquired a VCR, a tape recorder, a word processor—and I plunge myself into them, I read and study enthusiastically—I even have a workshop in the basement—"

"I've been told that Professor Russo was the English department's second choice for this tenured job. Is that true?"

"No doubt of it."

"Why was he the second choice? What did your department think was wrong with him?"

"Why, nothing at all. Mike is a splendid teacher. As a matter of fact, in terms of popularity with students, his classes have had substantially higher enrollments than Stu's classes. Though the academic enterprise, you understand, should never be turned into a popularity contest. As far as scholarship goes—publications and so on—Stu and Mike are pretty much equal.

"In the end, we had to make the choice on very elusive grounds, on a certain—well, call it a fit—between the man and the institution. Mike is first-rate, but there's just a smidgen, just the smallest element of—what shall I call it?—roughness about him. His edges haven't quite been polished as finely as Stu's. It's not Mike's fault, God knows—a man certainly isn't responsible for the kind of background he's been brought up in—but since we did have to choose—" Van Horn made a delicate little palm-spreading gesture.

"You told the two men about the department's decision, I suppose?"

"Oh, yes. I had them both into my office Tuesday afternoon. The day before the murder."

Which explained why Mike, at the poetry reading Tuesday night, had looked like a man who'd just had the roof cave in on him.

"As a matter of fact," Van Horn was going on, "this situation has presented me with a most perplexing quandary. Dean Bradbury has asked me to arrange a memorial service for Stu—it'll be held in the college chapel Saturday afternoon at two. His mother and his sister are flying in from Providence Friday night. Nothing religious, of course, in the denominational sense. Just some brief readings, by Stu's colleagues, from various literary works of an appropriate nature. My own contribution will be a few lines from Gray's 'Elegy.' The quandary is, should I or shouldn't I ask Mike Russo to join in on the service? Since he *is* going to be tried for poor Stu's murder, it might seem to be in rather poor taste— On the other hand, a man is assumed innocent until proven guilty, so if I leave him out of the service, won't it be interpreted as a prejudgment on my part—"

"I wonder if it's occurred to you," I said, "that Mike Russo might not be guilty?"

He blinked at me politely. "You think so?"

"Well, after all, since there *are* so many seething tensions in an academic community, why couldn't there be somebody besides Mike Russo who has a reason for killing Professor Bellamy? You don't happen to know of anybody like that, do you?"

"Somebody else with a motive? Now let me see. Stu, as I said, was always the gentleman, scrupulously polite and sociable. He wasn't the most *forthcoming* person in the world, of course. There may have been a certain lack of warmth, a certain reserve. But I hardly think it could've been sufficient to drive anyone to kill him—" He broke off, frowning harder. "There *was* that student, of course."

"What student?"

"It was several days ago—Monday afternoon, to be exact. Toward three o'clock, I was on my way out for the day, I passed Stu's office door. And I heard this terrible row from inside. Loud voices, raised in anger. One was Stu's voice, very deep, easily recognized. The other voice was high-pitched, definitely a young voice. It was difficult to make out what either of them was saying. Then the door of the office opened, and this boy came stamping out. Then he turned in the doorway, and I heard him yelling, 'You've got no right to do this to me! All those fancy things you're always saying, and you can still do something like this?'

"Stu made some kind of an answer. I could hear his deep voice, but once again I couldn't make out the words. It seemed to enrage the boy even more, and he yelled, 'You're going to be sorry for this!' And then he stamped over to the stairs and was gone. I stayed where

84

I was for a few moments longer, until Stu closed his door again—"

"They couldn't see you, where you were standing?"

"Oh, no, I ducked around the corner as Stu's office door opened. It would have been most embarrassing—for them—if they had realized they were overheard."

"What did the boy look like?"

"I never saw his face, his back was toward me throughout the whole scene. It didn't last very long, you understand. I could see the back of his neck, and I could see he had dark hair, and he was short, probably no more than five feet six or seven, and—yes, he wore an earring."

"In which ear?"

"Well, both of them, now that I think of it."

It flicked through my mind that this was definitely food for thought. But I had no time to chew it over at that moment.

"But this student wasn't familiar to you in any way? You didn't get the impression he was somebody you've had in class?"

"I'm truly sorry, I just can't say about that one way or another. Is that all you have to ask me? Well, then—"

Van Horn got to his feet, so I did too. "I certainly wish you luck in your investigations," he said. "Mike's case seems to be in good hands. If somebody else *did* kill Stu, I'm sure you'll find out who it was. I must say, I'm rather glad that the finger of suspicion can't possibly fall on me."

"Not that it has," I said, "but why do you think it can't?"

"Well, I couldn't have killed poor Stuart even if I had wanted to, could I? I was in my house, at my party, talking to him on the phone when he died. What's the popular expression again?" He gave his little cat laugh. "Yes. An airtight alibi."

CHAPTER 13

AFTER I LEFT Van Horn's office, I went down the corridor to see if anybody else I wanted to talk to was around. There was no light shining through any of the transoms. So I left the building and went back to my car in the Llewellyn Hall parking lot.

The snow was still coming down full force, and my car was loaded down with the stuff. It was four-thirty already, no point fighting this blizzard to drive back to my office. After brushing the snow off my windshield, I headed in the other direction, to my house. And I found Mom waiting for me, practically pushing a cup of hot coffee into my hands as I walked through the door.

Before I started drinking it, though, I checked in with Ann at the office. She was back from court, and told me, with a definite edge of satisfaction in her voice, that the judge had agreed to let Mike out on bail.

"We had a stroke of luck. The judge was Sam Winslow, he's a graduate of Mesa Grande College and also happens to have been an English major. George

Wolkowicz didn't like it too much. You would've enjoyed seeing his face."

"So Mike is out of jail now?" I asked.

"Free as a bird—until he goes on trial."

That made me happy. I had no idea how things would be for him at the college, but at least he wouldn't spend the next few months rotting in one of the county's cells. It's funny, in the days when I was a cop I sent people off to those cells by the hundreds and never gave it a second thought. Now that I'm on the other side of the fence, the very thought of such a place makes my blood boil.

I told Ann about the earring I'd found under Bellamy's bookcase, and about the student who was fighting with Bellamy and who also wore earrings. She just grunted noncommittally at all this. Wild bursts of optimism were never what you got from Ann. "Okay, follow it up," she said. "It certainly won't hurt."

She hung up, and I turned back to Mom, and saw that she had brought out a plate of *schnecken* for me to munch on while I drank my coffee. *Schnecken,* with nuts and raisins, sticky and delicious! I hadn't tasted anything like it since my last trip to New York.

"Mom, where did you find a bakery in town that makes things like this?"

"Who needs bakeries?" she said. "You've got an oven, and I had a little time after I got back from my bridge game."

Now I realized that the house was full of that lovely *schnecken*y smell. It filled the soul with contentment.

I sat back in my favorite easy chair in the living room, the coffee cup in my hand and a piece of *schnecken* in my other hand, and I asked Mom about her afternoon. She told me she'd had a nice couple of rubbers of bridge at the YMCA. Met some nice people, too, and one of them was picking her up tomorrow and, if the weather was better, showing her the mountains.

87

"But Mom, when you've seen one mountain, you've seen them all."

"That's true. But Mr. Bernstein's enthusiastic about them, and what's the point of hurting people's feelings?"

"Mr. Bernstein? You're going to the mountains tomorrow with a Mr. *Bernstein*?"

"You didn't think they had any out here? They've also got a synagogue, did you know that? I'll bet you never set foot in it, even on the High Holidays. Tomorrow night I'll be going out there for Shabbat. They asked me to make some chocolate-chip cookies for the reception afterward. You wouldn't like to join me for the services, maybe? Don't answer, I know already what you're going to say."

Mom talked a little more about Mr. Bernstein, who used to own a clothing store in town but sold out to a big chain a few years ago and was enjoying his retirement on the income. His wife had been dead for five years, and he had three grown daughters, all married and living in other parts of the country. He spent most of his time at bridge tournaments to keep from feeling lonely.

"Don't worry, don't worry," Mom said, evidently noticing something on my face. "Bernstein's a nice fellow, but definitely not my type. He's very sweet, if you follow me. That's the trouble, all that sweetness, I can take it in small doses but for a daily diet it would give me diabetes."

Social formalities were over now, and it was time for me to lay out the events of my afternoon for Mom. There's no such thing in this world as free *schnecken* and coffee. So I told her everything that had happened to me since my noontime lunch with her, and I showed her the little red earring.

Mom held it in her palm for a while, peering down at it. Then she handed it back to me, saying absolutely nothing at all.

"Well, what do you think?" I said. "Any chance we'll be able to trace the student from that?"

"Why shouldn't you trace him? You already got a good description of him."

"I don't see that at all. Van Horn didn't see his face and didn't recognize anything about him."

"Except he's got dark hair, and he's short—and he's a he."

"There are probably a few hundred students at the college who fit that description."

"And he's taking one of Bellamy's classes right now."

"How do you figure that, Mom?"

"Because he yelled at him, 'You've got no right to do this to me!' What can a professor do to a student unless the student is taking one of his classes? What other way has the professor got for putting pressure on the student? Outside the class the professor is nobody, inside the class he's Adolph Hitler."

"All right, let's assume this student is taking one of Bellamy's classes. The professors teach three courses per semester, that's anywhere from sixty to a hundred and fifty students. At least twenty or thirty of them will be short, dark males."

"Who wear earrings?"

"Lots of males wear earrings nowadays, especially college-age males. You'd be surprised, Mom."

"Surprised I wouldn't be. The way people behave stopped surprising me a long time ago. Anyway, you want to narrow it down a little more? How about that this student is a Chicano?"

"A Chicano!"

"This is what they're called out here, isn't it? People that are Mexican-Americans? If I've got the wrong expression—"

"The expression is right. But why should you assume the student is a Chicano?"

"You remember what he said to Bellamy, and Van Horn overheard it? 'All those fancy things you're always saying, and you can still do something like this? What did he mean? What fancy things? What was the professor always saying which seemed to contradict what he was doing to this boy?"

"Mom, we can't possibly know!"

"We *do* know. He was an expert on books about black people, he wrote articles on the subject—isn't that so? So wouldn't you naturally assume, a man who specializes in such a subject, who's always talking about it, who tries to get students to care about this type literature, he wouldn't be prejudiced against minorities himself? But to this student in his class he does something that looks like it's prejudiced, and the student is amazed and yells out, 'All those fancy things you're always saying, and you can still—'"

"Wait a second, Mom. It was *black* literature that Bellamy was an expert in. So why would you figure that the student who yelled those words is a Chicano? Isn't it more likely he'd be a black?"

"Maybe—only we've got other evidence he wasn't."

"What evidence?"

"Van Horn gave you a description what this young fellow looked like from the back. He saw his earring, his dark hair, the back of his neck. If this had been a black young fellow, wouldn't you expect Van Horn to mention it? So he wasn't black. So there's only one other oppressed minority that you have out here. Chicanos."

I thought it over for a few seconds and decided she had a point. The problem of digging up the mysterious student suddenly looked a lot simpler. All we had to do was go through Bellamy's current class lists and pick out the Mexican names. There couldn't be more than two or three of them, and if one of these people was short and dark haired, was having troubles in Bellamy's class, and

90

wore earrings—and if he turned out to have lost one of those earrings recently—

That was when the phone rang.

I picked it up, and a voice said my name.

"You're talking to him," I said. "Who is it?"

"Never mind who this is," said the voice, and I noticed now how peculiar it sounded. Low and muffled, as if it was talking through some thicknesses of cloth. I couldn't be sure if it was a man or a woman. "Have you seen what's on your front doorstep yet?"

"No—"

"Better go see," said the voice, and the phone clicked at the other end.

I went across the living room to the front door. A blast of cold air came at me as I opened it. The snow was still coming down, though a little less thickly than earlier, and the lawn gleamed white in the moonlight. On the doormat at my feet, sheltered from the snow by the arch of the doorway, was a white rectangular envelope.

I didn't see any footprints, either on the mat or coming up to the house from the sidewalk. There wouldn't be any, of course, if the envelope had been left there half an hour or more earlier; the snow would have covered them up.

I picked up the envelope and opened it in the hallway, as soon as I had shut the door against the cold.

The envelope itself had a printed return address in one corner: "Mesa Grande College." Inside it was a folded sheet of white paper, regulation typing size, and the message on it had been neatly typed on a word processor and printed out on a dot-matrix machine. I could check it in the morning, but I had a feeling the college was full of dot-matrix printers, every one of which produced characters that looked exactly like these. And since it was a common brand, there were thousands of them all over the city, too.

"So read it, read it," Mom said, bustling up to me in the hallway.

What I read began with my name and continued as follows:

> I am a student at this institution. Because I am usually broke, I supplement my income by doing a little pilfering. Last night I was going through the second floor of Llewellyn around ten o'clock when I made a very interesting discovery in one of the offices. I didn't understand what it meant when I ran across it, but this morning I read about Professor Bellamy's murder, and now I know what I've got.
>
> I've got conclusive evidence of who the murderer is.
>
> I'd like to give this evidence to you, because the public defender is handling Professor Russo's case, and this evidence will clear him. Of course you can't expect me to perform this civic duty without recompense. If you want to talk this over with me and come to some agreement on the terms, go to Manitou Park at midnight tonight. Sit down on the bench in front of General Wagner's elm tree, and I'll be in touch with you shortly.
>
> I'll talk only with you. If more than one person shows up, or if you tell the police about this, or if you have the park watched or make any other effort to find out who I am, the deal is off, and I'll throw my little discovery off a mountain.
>
> So please don't blow it.
>
> Sincerely yours,
> Zorro

"Zorro, what kind of name is that?" Mom said, returning to the rocker in the living room. "It could be some kind of nut, some kind of psychological killer—"

"More likely it's a college kid, and this is his idea of a joke."

She looked at me for a long time. A very familiar look. I had seen it often back in New York, from the day

I started working as a policeman. "You're going, I suppose?" she finally said.

I told her it was my job.

Another moment, then the look disappeared, and a smile took its place. "All this talking," she said, "I hope you worked up a good appetite. I'm giving you potted chicken for dinner."

CHAPTER
14

DURING THAT DINNER—a potted chicken that took me back to some of the happiest moments of my childhood—neither of us said a word about Manitou Park. Mom filled me in on the people she was close to back in New York—neighbors, friends, tradesmen. Some of them I'd known, some of them I hadn't, but her stories about them never failed to fascinate me. It's amazing the complicated and ingenious ways that human beings can think of to screw up their lives and everybody else's.

After dinner I did the dishes. Mom refused to let me at first, but I told her that my self-esteem as a member of the women's-lib generation would be severely damaged if she didn't. So she gave in, sighing and muttering about how men nowadays don't have any backbone like they used to have. This from a woman whose husband had been firmly under her thumb, with no hope of escape, throughout their entire married life!

When I was through with the dishes, I called Ann and told her about "Zorro." "Be careful," was all she said.

There were still a few hours to kill after that, so Mom and I played gin rummy. She was the one who had taught me the game, when I was a kid. She skunked me as easily as ever. I lost a dollar and eighty cents to her, and don't think she didn't make me fork over every penny. Mother love may be the most beautiful of all human sentiments, but Mom wasn't about to let it interfere with a legitimate gambling debt.

At a quarter of twelve, I put on my overcoat and my fur hat, wound a muffler around my neck, and went to the back door which led out of the kitchen, my car being stowed away in the garage behind the house. Mom went to the door with me.

"You'll be warm enough?" she said.

"I'll be fine."

"So—I'll see you later."

"Don't wait up for me, for God's sake," I said.

"You're a big boy, why should I wait up?"

The snow had stopped falling by now, but the cold cut through my clothing, and the heater in my car is one of its many parts that could use a lot of improvement. I got to Manitou Park a few minutes early, just to be on the safe side.

It's set in the middle of the downtown section of town, and all it covers is one square block. Inside it are swings and picnic tables and an area for horseshoes and shuffleboard, but not many children or horseshoe players ever use it, because in the last fifteen years it's turned into the local haven for hobos and hippies, a place where you can buy or sell all kinds of drugs at any time of day. The Downtown Merchants Association and other civic groups are always protesting about the degeneration of Manitou Park, and the cops occasionally announce they're staging a crackdown. But the day after the crackdown, go to the park and you'll find what you're looking for just as easily as before.

Now I have to admit it, this park is not a particularly

savory spot at midnight. All you can see in there are a few shadowy figures, and you should probably be grateful that you can't see their faces. I took a deep breath, said a little prayer to myself, and walked through the iron gateway.

Moving fast, I headed to the exact center of the square and stopped at the huge elm tree. It's known as General Wagner's elm tree because it was planted at that site—long before the park came into existence around it—by General William Henry Harrison Wagner, the hero of the Indian Wars who founded Mesa Grande in the 1880s. There's a bench right next to it, big enough for two people. I sat down on it, trying to ignore the bitter cold that was seeping into my bones.

The chimes from the clock at the Mesa Grande National Bank Building sounded twelve times, and at that exact same moment I felt a hand on my shoulder.

I came close to jumping to my feet with a yelp, but a voice spoke sharply into my ear. "Shut up. Don't turn around."

The same voice I'd heard earlier over the phone. Low and muffled, talking through cloth.

I said, "This is going to be pretty tough if I can't—"

A sharp jab in the back of my neck discouraged me from going on. Then a hand, with a thick glove on it, reached over my shoulder and thrust a piece of paper into my face.

I took it and read it, squinting in the dim light. It was written on the same word processor as the earlier letter, and it said:

> I've got what you need. It proves Russo didn't do the murder. I could get two or three hundred bucks for it from my usual sources. But I want something else.
> Russo has a book. *The Collected Poems of Emily Dickinson,* the first collection that was published in America. It's a first edition. I've seen it. The cover is

damaged, a lot of the pages are dog-eared, it's not that rare, probably not worth too much. Russo says it's the only valuable book he owns.

I want it. I'll trade him for it.

I looked up from the letter. "How are we supposed to know this so-called evidence of yours will really do us any good? If you'd give me some idea of what it is—"

I started to turn around, then felt two hands clamping over both my ears and gripping hard as they snapped my head to the front again. It wasn't a pleasant sensation.

This little punishment was administered in absolute silence. Then one of the gloved fingers pointed at the letter, and I understood I was being ordered to go on reading.

I'll give you two days. Meet me here again, Saturday at midnight, same conditions. No cops. No smart-ass tricks.

You bring what I want, I'll bring what you want.

Don't cross me up.

Captain Blood

"Hey! What're you two doing there?"

I made out a voice, calling from a distance. It had to be a cop.

The hand clamped down on my shoulder again, not very gently.

"Don't get paranoid," I said. "I came here alone, I didn't bring the cops. They patrol this park from time to time, you know."

The hand lifted from my shoulder, and I could hear footsteps scrambling away behind me. I also heard the rustling of leaves and branches. Captain Blood, formerly Zorro, was hotfooting it into the bushes.

I just had time to shove the letter into my coat pocket when a patrolman in uniform came lumbering up to me.

Only it wasn't a him, I realized, it was a her. In her

97

thirties, short, stocky, and muscular, with a permanently unbelieving expression on her face.

"I lost my wallet here earlier today," I said. "I was hoping it might still be here."

"Who's the guy that was just with you?"

"Never saw him before. He was sitting here, and he helped me look for it. I guess you scared him away." I tried to make my voice casual. "You got a good look at the guy, did you?"

"In this light? All I saw was a hat and a long overcoat." She kept peering at me for a while, then she said, "It all sounds pretty fishy to me. But I haven't got anything on you, so get the hell out of here. This is no place to hang around in, night *or* day."

"Thank you, Officer, good night," I said, and moved away from her as fast as I could.

Driving home, shivering in the freezing cold, I tried to figure out what had actually happened, who the mysterious voice belonged to, what it all meant anyhow. I couldn't come to any conclusions at all.

It was almost one o'clock when I got back to my house. Mom was still up, rocking.

"So you want a nice cup of tea, a drink, maybe?"

Tea sounded good. While I drank it and my bones thawed out, I told her what had happened to me in the park.

"And you didn't get even one quick look at who it was?"

"Not a chance," I said. "I can't even tell you if it was a man or a woman. And the voice spoke only a few words."

Mom shook her head. "I don't like it when people act that way."

"What way?"

"Unselfish. Like they're not interested in money. This person you just met in the park—Captain Blood?

98

Zorro?—it's supposed to be a student who makes ends meet by doing a little stealing on the side, right?"

"That's what he wrote in his letter."

"So is it common with students these days, I wonder, they prefer a rare book to three hundred dollars in cash? And a book they won't even be able to tell people about or sell, a book they'll have to keep hidden away? Such a love of literature yet! This generation of students is certainly different from the ones that were around when you went to college."

"Okay, it's unusual. But it did happen. So what's the explanation?"

"At this time of night, who has explanations? Personally I'm going to bed. You should go to bed, too, you need your sleep, you're a growing—" She stopped herself in the middle of the old formula, with an embarrassed little grin.

CHAPTER 15

IN THE MORNING Mom made pancakes—light, thin buttermilk pancakes. I wallowed in a sense of childish contentment. I wondered if it was good for my character. For about three seconds I wondered, then I had some more pancakes.

I asked her what she was doing today, and she reminded me that Mr. Bernstein, the retired clothing-store owner, would be picking her up shortly, and since the weather seemed to be nice again he would drive her up into the mountains. It occurred to me I should phone the office that I'd be late, so I could wait around and get a look at Bernstein. After all, Mom was an old lady, in a strange place surrounded by strange people, and I was the only protection she had in the world.

I pushed that foolish thought away pretty damned quick. Mom could take care of herself. From the day of her birth.

I left the house right after breakfast, and at nine o'clock Ann and I met Mike Russo in her office. She had called him first thing this morning to set up the meeting.

He was looking drawn and anxious, and who could blame him? Nobody wants to be the star attraction in a murder trial. Especially in a town like Mesa Grande, where the newspaper hasn't got much else of local interest to titillate the sadistic impulses of the citizenry.

Not that murder is all that rare out here. We've got an army camp outside of town, a red-light district, an above-average rate of unemployment, a thriving trade in illegal chemical substances: Proportionately, we produce at least as much blood and gore per year in the shadow of the Rockies as my old hometown produces in the shadow of the Empire State Building. But *this* kind of murder we're not used to. Nice respectable people, college professors, upstanding members of the middle class, bashing one another over the head. The *Republican-American* would have it on the front page for the next week, and the headlines would burst out all over again when the trial began.

I started off our conference with an account of my conversation with Van Horn and his story about the student who had threatened Bellamy. I explained why it seemed to me this student was probably a Chicano. (I didn't bother to attribute my logic to Mom, I'm afraid, but of course she never wants to take the credit.) Then I described my encounter with the mysterious student-thief last night. When I came to the part about *The Collected Poems of Emily Dickinson,* Mike gave a little gasp. "Son of a bitch!" he said.

"This Zorro claims to have seen your book," Ann said. "How many people have you ever shown it to? If we could narrow it down—"

"I've shown it to a lot of people, I'm afraid," Mike said. "When I teach Emily Dickinson—and I teach her poetry in three or four classes every year—I always bring the book in to let my students look at it."

"What about your colleagues in the English department, have any of them ever seen it?"

"I've shown it to most of them."

"How did you happen to get hold of it in the first place?"

"I ran across it in a secondhand store in New Haven. Six or seven years ago, when I was still in grad school. I was browsing in there, and I saw 'First Edition' on the flyleaf, and the store was selling it for some ridiculously low price, so I grabbed it."

"Any idea what it's really worth?"

"A few hundred dollars maybe—that's what a rare-book dealer here in town told me. But it doesn't matter. I'm never going to sell it." His face grew a little paler than before. "And I'm not going to give it away either. Not to some crummy extortionist."

"Not even," Ann said, "if that's the only way to get yourself out from under this murder charge?"

"Well, we don't know that, do we? This may be some kind of con game, this Zorro person may be lying. But even if he isn't, even if he really *has* some evidence that can help me—I'm damned if he's getting that book out of me! It means a lot to me, and I'm just not going to throw it away!"

He stopped talking, then he lowered his eyes, and his voice was a lot less determined. "Besides, there's a good chance, isn't there, that we won't need this evidence this Zorro claims he's got? I mean, the Chicano student who was fighting with Stu, isn't that a pretty promising lead?"

"Most leads don't keep their promises," Ann said.

She let this sink in until Mike's face was properly crestfallen. Then she stood up. "You're the client, it's your decision. We'll just have to do the best we can."

102

CHAPTER 16

I HAD A LOT of morning ahead of me, so I decided to go up to the college and get Bellamy's current class lists from the registrar. I intended to pick out all the Mexican-sounding names from those lists, track those people down, and find out if any of them could be the student who yelled at Bellamy in his office last Monday.

I drove up to the college, taking it slow and easy, because last night's snow was freezing on the streets and my car is a great little skidder. The sun was bright, and the white was sparkling from lawns and roofs and treetops. And the mountains, when you glimpsed them from the ends of the cross streets, looked like white-haired giants. Patriarchs from some old-fashioned illustrated edition of the Bible. On a day like this, it wasn't quite as hard as usual to understand why the people in this area are so obsessed with God, get such a kick out of honking for Jesus.

Llewellyn Hall seemed deserted as I climbed the stairs to the second floor. Classes were in progress, and everyone was inside the classrooms, I supposed, hanging on their teacher's words—or hanging on their own yawns. The registrar's office was in the front of the building, and I started in that direction. But then I got a better idea.

It was nearly half past ten. Classes wouldn't break for twenty-five minutes or so. Stuart Bellamy's office was just a few yards down the hall. His current class lists would undoubtedly be in that office somewhere. And other things—who knew what?—might be in that office too. And in my pocket, suddenly feeling very heavy, was this bunch of keys I always carry. Very useful, versatile keys.

I hurried down the hall to Bellamy's office, took a quick look over my shoulder to make sure nobody was in sight, and started trying keys in the door. The third one worked.

Shutting the door behind me, I took a few seconds just to look over the room, get some feel for it. It was very different from the living room in Bellamy's house, where his body had been lying. There were no books in this office at all. Bare shelves and just a couple of neat piles of paper on the desk. The walls were undecorated except for a blown-up framed photograph of Scott Fitzgerald. A famous photograph, with the head tossed back, the hair unruly, the shirt open at the collar: the Author as Every Schoolgirl's Romantic Dream.

Everything else about this office suggested that Bellamy didn't spend much of his time here, so why did he keep the photograph here, why not back at his house with his books, his Hemingway, his Faulkner?

The answer, I decided, was that he had to spend *some* time in this office, talking to students, whether he liked it or not. And it had been necessary to him, during those hours of enforced drudgery, to have this image on the wall to look at now and again. To identify with maybe?

I looked through the piles of papers on his desk. Nothing significant about any of them. Xeroxed notices from the college mostly. About as impersonal as you could get. But one of the piles had what I was looking for, three official class lists, printed out from the registrar's computer. English 104: Introductory Fiction. English 332: The Nineteenth-Century American Novel. English 333: The Twentieth-Century American Novel.

There were about eighty or ninety names among the three lists, and three of them looked Mexican to me. One of these three was a woman—Bertha Alvarez, a freshman. The other two were men—Luis Vallejos, a sophomore (The Nineteenth-Century American Novel), and Tomas Trujillo, a senior (The Twentieth-Century American Novel). And the registrar couldn't have been kinder and more accommodating to a hardworking investigator: After each name was a phone number.

The number after Luis Vallejos' name was a private phone in town, the number after Tomas Trujillo's name was an extension in one of the college dorms. So I used the phone in Bellamy's office to call that extension. A tired male voice answered after seven or eight rings: Somebody had had a long, hard night. I asked for Tomas Trujillo, and the voice said, "I'm his roommate, he isn't in right now. I think he's at basketball practice."

"He's on the basketball team?"

"That's right. You want to leave a message?"

"Never mind." I hung up the phone. The short slight boy that Van Horn had described wasn't on anybody's basketball team.

I was about to dial the college operator for an outside line to Luis Vallejos' number when I heard a noise. It was coming from about two inches away from me, it seemed. Then I realized it was coming from the office on my left. Somebody moving around in there, opening and closing a drawer. These walls were as thin as paper.

Whose office was it next door anyway? I shut my eyes and tried to visualize the corridor, with the names. It was

Samantha Fletcher's office. What was she doing here now when she ought to be teaching a class?

Then I heard another noise, which answered my question. The buzzer that signals the end of class, coming at me faintly from the corridor. I had no problem recognizing it: How many hours during my own college days had my whole heart and soul and mind been fixed on waiting for that buzzer?

I waited in Bellamy's office—cowered might be more accurate, because I could imagine the field day our district attorney would have if I were caught breaking and entering!—until I heard the door to Fletcher's office open and close.

I waited another few seconds, then I slipped out of Bellamy's office. Out in the corridor I found myself caught in the grand stampede of prisoners let loose from their confinement.

I moved with the flow down the stairs. The people around me, all of them young and full of beans, were yelling and laughing and arguing and giggling. None of them had the slightest idea that Jimmy Valentine, the Gentleman Cracksman, was in their midst.

CHAPTER 17

AFTER MY HAIRBREADTH ESCAPE from Llewellyn Hall, I went to the drugstore across the street from the campus and asked to see their phone book. I looked up Vallejos. There was a whole column of them, but the number I was looking for, the number that had been printed after Luis Vallejos' name on Bellamy's class list, was near the top. Carlos Vallejos. As I had thought, the kid was living at home with his family.

I decided to go right over there, without calling up first. Maybe nobody would be there, but if somebody was, it could be a great advantage to catch them by surprise, to talk to them before they had a chance to fix up a story.

Carlos Vallejos and his family lived on Cedar Street, not the slums by any means—a very respectable neighborhood, in fact—but definitely lower grade Mesa Grande. It was mostly Chicanos who lived here, with a sprinkling of enlisted men who had families and were on the permanent staff of the army base. The houses were all small, and the lawns were even smaller, but the snowplows, I noticed, *had* visited the neighborhood. In Mesa Grande the Chicano population votes.

The Vallejos house had a tiny porch, old, worn, not recently painted, but spotlessly clean. And the three or four shrubs in front of the house gave evidence of being carefully clipped and pruned. I rang the doorbell and waited a long time, and then a young man opened the door. He was small, dark, and slightly built, about nineteen or twenty. He was wearing a black leather jacket, sleek sideburns, and an undulating hairdo. His eyes were fixed on me with suspicion and hostility.

"What do you want?"

"I'm with the public defender's office—"

"You don't want me," he said. "You want my mother and father. They're at the restaurant, with the young ones, they won't be back till late this afternoon."

I asked him what he meant by the restaurant, and he explained that his parents owned a small place that served Mexican food. His mother was the cook, his father was the manager and headwaiter, his brothers and sisters helped out.

"But you don't help out?" I asked.

"I been working there since I was six years old, man," he said, flushing just a little. "But I got a different job now, at the gas station. It pays a lot better. I have to be there in a couple of hours."

All this time he didn't budge from the doorway.

"Can I come in?" I said. "It *is* you I want, as a matter of fact. I'm investigating the charges against Professor Russo, and I think you may be able to help me."

"I don't know anything about that professor. I never had any classes with him. I wouldn't know him if I saw him."

"You've been taking a course from Professor Bellamy, the one who got killed, haven't you?"

He looked at me hard, his long eyelashes hardly

flickering. Finally he said, "What's that got to do with anything, man?"

"Maybe the fight you had with him has something to do with something. Maybe the way he was screwing you over—"

I let my voice get louder, and he darted a couple of nervous glances out at the street in both directions. "Okay, man, you might as well come in."

I went in, and found myself in a small parlor with a couch and a few wicker chairs, all of this decorated in bright patterns. It was the kind of stuff that shows up on our local TV stations in advertisements for furniture sales.

The boy waved at one of the wicker chairs, and I sat down in it. He sat down on the couch, across from me, swinging one leg over the other, putting on a carefully bored expression and scratching his left ear. In the other ear, I noticed, he was wearing an earring, a small glitter of red glass. Offhand it looked like the same kind of earring I'd found under the bookcase in Bellamy's living room. I wondered if he had ever had a pair of them.

"You're saying I had some kind of fight with this Bellamy dude?" he said, keeping up the casual manner.

"In his office, a couple of days ago. You yelled at him for what he'd done to you and told him he'd be sorry. You were overheard when you threatened him."

"Threat! What threat? You lose your temper at somebody, who says that means you're going to do anything to hurt him?"

"The people who overheard you are prepared to swear it was a definite threat. And it happened just a few days before somebody killed him."

"That Russo dude killed him! The one you're working for! You want to get him off the hook by framing *me*!"

"Nobody's framing anybody. But sooner or later, you're going to have to explain what that fight was all

109

about. Tell me about it now, and maybe the public defender won't have to squeeze it out of you in court."

He chewed his lip angrily, then he shook his head and muttered, "Shit!" Then he said, "This Bellamy, he had it in for me, man. A week ago he gives us this exam, and it's important. You know, like if I flunk it, that son of a bitch could flunk me for the whole course. So we sat in the classroom and wrote in these blue books, and last Friday he gave them back to us. And he flunked me."

"Was it a tough exam?"

"It was a pisser. One big long essay, you had two hours to do it. You had a choice, from three different questions. I did the one about Nathaniel Hawthorne's political ideas. I proved this Hawthorne dude was a real activist. He didn't like what was going on in his shitty society—it was worse than what we've got today, only there wasn't any anti-Chicano prejudice then. There wasn't any Chicanos, right?"

"So he didn't like your essay and he flunked you," I said. "What did you do then?"

"First thing I did, right after class, I showed this essay to this friend of mine. She's smart, she knows a lot about literature and Nathaniel Hawthorne and what these English-professor dudes are looking for. She told me it was a good essay, it deserved at least an A-minus. And why not? I knew that stuff cold. I'll tell you a crazy thing, I even *like* this Hawthorne dude. So the other afternoon, I went to see this Bellamy cocksu—Professor Bellamy at his office, I asked him how come he flunked me."

"Then what?"

"I sat there in his office and told him I thought my exam was pretty good, and other people thought so, too, and would he explain why it deserved to be flunked. I didn't lose my temper. I was real polite. So what did that son of a bitch do? He laughed at me. A great big fucking horselaugh. He told me he didn't care what I thought or what any girlfriend of mine thought about my essay. *His*

110

opinion was what counted. *He* was saying I deserved to flunk, and that's all there was to it.

"So I still didn't lose my temper. Though I'm telling you, man, I was getting pretty close. I said I understood all that, his opinion was what counted, but he still didn't tell me what was wrong with my essay. So he laughed again, and he said there was no point telling me, because I couldn't understand anyway, and then he said he had other appointments, so I should get the hell out of his office. He went to the door and opened it, and I started to leave, but I yelled at him a little before I left."

"Why would he flunk you unless he thought you deserved it?"

"Oh, come on. You know what it is. He's a racist. He doesn't like Chicanos, he thinks we don't have any right in his classroom learning about Nathaniel Hawthorne, he thinks we should stay in the kitchen where we belong, making tortillas and sticking knives in each other. And I don't keep my mouth shut in class either. I don't agree with something he says, I tell him so."

"Did he ever make any racist remarks to you?"

"Every time he looks at me it's a racist remark."

"Did he ever actually use any racist language, in class maybe, when other people might have heard?"

"He's too smart for that. In class he's just a lily-white liberal, his heart bleeds for us disadvantaged, he loves the Third World, he says isn't it terrible nobody ever paid any attention before to this wonderful literature by blacks and Chicanos. He doesn't come out with anything in front of witnesses. But that doesn't change anything, man. That big fucking collection of books he's got—hundreds of them, all the way up to the ceiling—but none of it means a damn thing!"

I said nothing for a couple of seconds but didn't take my eyes off his face. Silence has a way of making people feel uneasy. Finally I said, "Where were you Wednesday night, when Professor Bellamy got killed?"

111

He didn't even blink at this. Either because the question presented no problems for him, or because he'd been steeling himself for it. "What time was that when he got killed?"

"At five minutes to eight."

"I was eating dinner then."

"At home, with your family?"

"No, I was out at a restaurant."

"From when to when?"

"I don't know exactly. Lemme think. Yeah, I must've got there around six-thirty, stayed there maybe a couple hours. Then I came straight home, and I was right here the rest of the night. Maybe from eight-thirty on."

"But at five to eight you were still in the restaurant?"

"That's it. I know that because I looked at the clock in there and set my watch by it."

"What restaurant?"

"This joint."

"What's the name of it? Where is it?"

"Who knows? I wasn't even paying attention. I got hungry, I went into this joint. The kind of place it was, maybe it didn't even *have* a name."

"What did you have to eat?"

"Like some kind of spaghetti."

"Who had dinner with you?"

"I was alone."

"You went out to eat in a restaurant all by yourself? You want me to believe that a sharp guy like you didn't have a date?"

"Why not? Sometimes you want to be alone." He put on a grin. "You get tired of the broads chasing after you all the time."

"How come you didn't have to work at the gas station that night?"

"Because I didn't start that job yet. I was still working at my old man's restaurant, I didn't start at the gas station until today. As a matter of fact, I broke it to the old

112

man at lunch that day, I told him I was quitting. He was pretty mad—"

"The reason you took the gas station job, it's because you need the extra money?"

"You ever hear of anybody who doesn't?"

"You didn't think you needed it so much for the last year or so, since you started college. You've been satisfied to help out in the restaurant. What happened a few weeks ago to change your mind?"

"Nothing happened. I just got sick and tired, working for my old man, working for peanuts."

"Is it a girl? Some new girlfriend who's costing you a lot?"

He shifted his eyes away. "There's no girl."

"You're sure about that? She isn't somebody who knows a lot about literature, so she could read your exam and tell you it didn't deserve a failing grade?"

"I make up my own mind! She never—"

"Who never?"

He muttered into his lap, "Nobody."

"If you need money so badly, why did you go out to a restaurant Wednesday night? Wasn't that pretty extravagant, when you could've eaten at home?"

"I told you that already. The old man was mad at me, we both did a lot of yelling that afternoon. So I felt like being alone."

"Can you prove that?"

"What do I have to prove? You're the one that has to prove. It's a democratic country, right? I'm innocent till you prove I'm guilty."

Just then the front door opened, and a girl came in. She was short and slim, with a lot of long dark hair. Her resemblance to Luis was striking, though she seemed to be about three years older.

"What's going down? Who's this?" She waved her arm at me angrily.

Luis answered her with a long tirade in Spanish, and

113

she tiraded back at him. Then she turned to me. "What're you bothering him for? Coming into people's houses and making accusations at them, what's the idea?"

I told her my name and what my job was, but I wasn't sure she had even bothered to hear me.

"I'm his sister Flora," she said. "Anything you want to accuse him of, you say it in front of me."

Her eyes were burning. From the corner of one of mine, I could see Luis sitting back on the couch, giving a big smirk.

"I'm waiting," she said. "You don't have anything you want to say? That's what I thought! Luis is a good boy, he never got in trouble in his whole life, not with the police, not with anybody else. He always got good grades in school, and they gave him this scholarship at the college, and his first year he had a B-plus average."

I thought about putting in a word or two, but she was all wound up, blasting down the track. It could have been dangerous to get in her way.

"Harvard College wanted him too, but they wouldn't give him the room and board, only the tuition. Here at Mesa Grande he can live at home. And all his life he worked hard, helped out Mama and Papa in the restaurant since he was a kid—the restaurant isn't such a big place, not many tables, but Mama makes the best sopapillas in town."

"I'd like to try them someday," I said, carefully not mentioning my true feelings about Mexican food. Everybody in this section of the country goes into ecstasies over Mexican food; it's safer to insult God than to say anything against enchiladas. "But that's got nothing to do with why I came here this morning."

"What're you waiting for, anyway? Tell me—*why* did you come here this morning?"

"To find out where Luis was at five minutes to eight

114

two nights ago, Wednesday night the twenty-third of March."

"That's when the professor got killed?"

"On the dot."

She glared at me a long time, then slowly the angry look faded from her face and was replaced by a smile. A friendly, almost insinuating smile which I didn't believe in for a minute. "Why didn't you say so in the first place? Five minutes to eight Wednesday night the twenty-third? Luis was with me."

I stared at her hard and said, "You're positive of that? You couldn't be thinking of some other night?"

"No other night. It was when the regular waitress, Rosa, called in sick, so I quit my job early to wait tables at the restaurant."

"What's your job?"

"I'm a beautician. I'm in the beauty parlor up at The Richelieu."

The beauty shop at The Richelieu is a major enterprise. It's patronized largely by the wives of Texas oilmen, California movie men, and other assorted millionaires who make this hotel their home away from home.

"What time were you working at the restaurant Wednesday?" I asked.

"I filled in from five to nine-thirty. And Papa and Mama were out in the kitchen all that time, too. In case you're thinking *they* need an alibi."

"A lot of people saw you there that night?"

"We don't have room for more than five tables. Four of them were full that night, so that's maybe ten, twelve, people that saw me."

"Regular customers? They know who you are?"

"All regular customers. I'll give you their names and addresses. It's a family place, a neighborhood place."

"And those people also saw Luis?"

115

She shrugged. "Maybe not. He pulled up in the car, gave a honk for me, and I went out to talk to him."

"What about?"

"This fight he had with Papa. How he could make it up."

"You knew about it already by then?"

"Luis told me about it earlier. Around five o'clock or so, when I got home from the beauty shop. He was waiting for me outside the house, he wouldn't go inside because he didn't want to see Papa. He asked me what should he do about the fight, and I told him I'll think about it. And he said he was going out for dinner, and he needed my car, my VW bug."

"You let him take it?"

"Sure I let him take it. As long as I was waiting tables that night, I wouldn't be going anywhere. But he was back again by a quarter of eight, the latest, ten of. He honked the horn from the street, and I came out, and we sat in the car and talked for half an hour, maybe longer."

"What about?"

"His fight with Papa. I was trying to tell him, he should be nice and apologize. But they're both a couple of stubborn—"

"You weren't missed in the restaurant?"

"Mama and Papa could handle it in there. They thought I just went to the john."

"Luis just told me he didn't got back from dinner till eight-thirty. How come you put it forty-five minutes earlier?"

Before she could answer that, Luis spoke up. "Hey, wait a second! I just remembered, my watch was running fast on Wednesday. If it said eight-thirty, the right time must've been a quarter of."

"Didn't you tell me you set your watch that night from the clock in the restaurant?"

"Did I say that? I got mixed up with a different night,

116

man. It was a couple months ago when I set my watch from a clock in a restaurant."

He was grinning practically ear to ear. It wasn't a grin I liked very much.

His sister pushed forward. "All right, you get out now," she said to me. "I don't want you around in case Mama and Papa come home. You're not going to get them upset."

So I got to my feet. "Thanks for your help," I said, and suddenly turned to Luis. "I'd like to ask you just one more question. What happened to your other earring?"

His hand flew up to his left ear, and his face flushed. Then, quick, he gave his sarcastic laugh. "What're you talking about, man? One earring is all I wear."

"Get out, get out!" his sister cried, practically shoving me through the front door.

CHAPTER 18

SINCE I HADN'T GOT around to Samantha Fletcher yesterday, I decided that my next step was to talk to her. But I drove back to the office first. Ann was there, so I told her about my interview with the Vallejoses, brother and sister.

At the end of my report, Ann gave her noncommittal grunt. She'd rather die than show she was either upset or overjoyed about something. "So there goes our substitute for Mike Russo."

"I don't see that at all," I said. "Isn't it obvious the sister is lying? She'd do anything for her brother, and especially to save her mother and father from grief. If I do a little digging into that alibi she's giving him—"

"Where are you going to begin?" Ann said. "You can bet she was working at her parents' restaurant Wednesday night—she wouldn't tell you that if it couldn't be confirmed. She was in and out all night long, nobody's going to remember if they missed her for half an hour or so. Okay, she can't prove she talked to her brother in his car at five of eight, but *we* can't prove she didn't."

"Maybe you could break her down on the witness stand."

"Come on, Dave, that's strictly from "Perry Mason." You know as well as I do, any case that depends on breaking somebody down on the witness stand—unless you start off with a lot of solid facts to do the breaking with—is doomed from the start. Besides, how are we going to get her on the witness stand in the first place? The prosecution sure won't call her, and the only way we could call her would be to lay some foundation ahead of time that her testimony is relevant to our case. It doesn't do us a bit of good to prove Luis Vallejos has no alibi for the time of the murder. The world is *full* of people who have no alibi for the time of the murder. What we have to do is place him there, squarely on the spot—the way the tire marks of Russo's car place *him* there. And I'm damned if I know how we're going to manage that."

"So what are you going to do?"

"One thing I'll do is give our client a call. Try to make him see reason about that Emily Dickinson book of his. That mysterious character in the park looks to me like our only bet right now."

"You'll let me know how it turns out?"

She said she would, and I returned to my cubbyhole.

For the rest of the morning I tried off and on to get hold of Samantha Fletcher. She didn't answer her office phone till just before lunchtime. When I told her who I was and what I wanted, she said she'd have a cocktail with me this afternoon. Could I meet her somewhere at four?

I suggested The Snuggery, which is one of several rooms at The Richelieu. Each of these rooms caters to a different taste: pretentious French, cozy old-fashioned American, swinging discoland, and so forth. The Snuggery is for those who feel the need to be English. It looks like a London pub and serves steak-and-kidney pie and Guinness stout. On the walls are framed posters that

119

show the Thames at sunrise and Westminster Abbey at night, and the piped-in music features the voices of Noël Coward, Gracie Fields, the Beatles, and other British icons. It's even possible, in one corner of the bar, to play darts.

All of this isn't cheap, but after all it was on the taxpayer.

The Snuggery is usually crowded, and especially in the late afternoon, during the cocktail hour. Fletcher was there ahead of me, and as I approached her, sitting alone at the table, I got the definite impression that there were tears in her eyes. But they were gone by the time I sat down across from her.

The waitress came over to us. Fletcher glared through her thick glasses and said, "I'll have a bottle of beer. Ordinary light-colored American beer. None of this thick black English muck, okay?"

I ordered the same, and the waitress said, "Amazing," and went off.

"Did you hear that word?" Fletcher said. "'Amazing.' That's strictly a Mesa Grande word, pure middle America. For sheer inanity I rank it right up there with 'neat' and 'real.' As in 'She's a real human being!'"

The waitress brought our beers, and Fletcher took a long loud gulp. Then she turned her attention to me.

"You're defending Mike Russo, are you? I hope you don't think he's guilty!"

"He isn't?"

"*Obviously* he isn't. It's typical of this crazy town that anyone should think he did it, even for a moment."

"He does seem to have a pretty strong motive."

"Motive! Okay, I admit it, this whole screwy tenure business is practically an invitation for people to cut each other's throats. I mean, it would turn Saint Francis into a cynic."

"How come?"

"Because it's so damned hypocritical, that's how

120

come. You spend three years or so of your life as a graduate student—which is another word for slave. You correct papers, teach three hours a day, pour on the flattery, generally break your ass so the Distinguished Professors can grind out their scholarly blather, in between sets of tennis. All of this so someday you, too, can achieve tenure, be a Distinguished Professor, and play tennis yourself. And what happens when you finally get out of graduate school and become a doctor of philosophy? They give you something to be philosophical *about*—they tell you there are no jobs available.

"Or worse still, they put you on a tenure track, you waste another six years of your life, and then you find out there's only *one* job available and somebody else is going to get it. Who could blame poor Mike if his thoughts turned to murder?"

"So you *are* saying Mike Russo may have killed Bellamy?"

"I'm not saying anything of the kind. All I said was, who could blame him? But the fact of the matter is, Mike Russo just isn't the murdering type. He's too much of a—a—" She groped in the air for the word. "—A believer! He actually believes that what he's doing matters. He believes he can make the world a better place by pumping literature into those hard little heads. It sounds corny, I suppose, but Mike is on the side of life, not death."

She took a swig of beer and looked around at her surroundings. She made a face. "God, how can you stand this place? All these turtleneck sweaters and ascots!"

"You don't like it?" I said. "It's a big hangout for independent-minded women who are making careers for themselves."

"And not one of them would be seen dead here without a man! Look at that table in the corner—why are those women laughing their heads off at the joke that guy just made? You can tell from the fatuous grin on his face it must've been a stinker. Independent minded! What's the use of a woman going out into the world and making a career if she just lets her office be turned into another kitchen?"

"Tell me about Van Horn's party," I said. "What time did you get there, what did you do before the phone call came?"

"Well, let me see. I got to Marcus' place around seven-forty-five. I was a little late, but I had to have a big dinner first, because I knew our beloved chairman isn't the man to provide a groaning board. Ritz crackers, pretzels, and that dreary slop he claims to put rum into—that's Marcus Van Horn's idea of lavish hospitality for his departmental serfs.

"Well, you were the first person I ran into, and while we were talking the phone rang, and a minute or so later I went out to the foyer and talked to Stu."

"That was in the middle of a crowd of people, lots of noise and confusion. Can you be absolutely sure it *was* Bellamy you were talking to?"

"You think it could've been somebody imitating his voice? Not a chance. I'd know that Stu Bellamy superior drawl anywhere."

"Van Horn says Bellamy's manner was strange. Abrupt, almost rude. Wouldn't let you get a word in."

"What was so strange about *that*? That's exactly how Stu talked to most people—that is, *he* did the talking and *you* did the listening. Marcus Van Horn thinks it's strange because Stu was very careful never to keep *him* from getting a word in. Stu knew what side his tenure bread was buttered on."

"In other words, he was a pretty self-centered type?"

"Oh, he tried to give the opposite impression. That eager, earnest all-American-boy manner he put on. Looking you in the eyes and saying, 'Tell me about yourself,' as if no subject on earth could possibly interest him

122

more. But you wouldn't get five words out of your mouth before he'd start telling you about himself."

"Were you surprised when he called you up at the party and read to you from that book?"

"Surprised! I was flabbergasted! Stu Bellamy voluntarily eating crow—that's a miracle I never expected to happen!"

"Did it seem especially miraculous on account of his condition?"

"What condition?"

"He had the flu, he was feeling terrible—"

"Flu!" She gave a sharp laugh. "He was faking it! He had this article to finish up by the end of the week, and Marcus Van Horn's parties bored him to tears anyway."

"How can you be so sure he was faking?"

"He told me so himself. The day before, it must've been around three in the afternoon, I came in to his office to ask him something about an advisee of mine who was in his Twentieth-Century American Novel class. The kid's also in Mike's poetry class, and Mike's office is in the same row as mine and Stu's, but I could hear Mike's typewriter going so I didn't want to disturb him. Anyway, as I was leaving Stu's office, I mentioned I'd be seeing him at Van Horn's the next night, and he said something like, 'Oh my God, I forgot all about the damn thing!' And then he said he was doing this article for one of the literary reviews, and he had to finish it before the end of the week."

"Did he say what magazine he was doing it for?"

"I don't remember. These days every third college in America publishes some kind of scholarly rag that nobody reads except the people who write for it and the people who are gunning for them. So he said he was going to call Marcus up the next day and tell him he had the flu, and I wouldn't give away his guilty secret, would I?"

123

"Did he let anybody else in on this guilty secret?"

"He said he wasn't going to." She gulped her drink, plucked up a pretzel, and popped it into her mouth.

"Suppose we get back to the tenure decision," I said. "Who did you vote for, Russo or Bellamy?"

"Good God, you don't think they'd let us lowly untenured worms cast a vote, do you? I can tell you who I *would've* voted for. Mike is ten times the teacher and scholar that Stu ever was."

"One more question," I said. "Who do *you* think did it? Was there anybody on the faculty, for instance, that Bellamy was particularly close to?"

"People don't get close in the academic world," she said. "You live right on top of each other, you see each other every day of your lives, but that doesn't mean anybody actually gives a damn about anybody else. What you give a damn about is your specialty. Your discipline, as they like to call it nowadays. Keeping up with your field—that doesn't leave you any time for people. Take me, for instance. I'm a medievalist. The castration of Abelard means a hell of a lot more to me than the murder of Stuart Bellamy."

"What about students? Do you know of any who might've had it in for Bellamy?"

She turned her head and waved her empty beer glass at the waitress. "Another bottle over here!" Then she turned back to me. "Students didn't like him much. And the feeling was mutual. But I don't think any of them would kill him for that."

"You don't know anything, then, about a student who's in one of his classes now? Short, thin, dark-haired boy. Wears earrings. Bellamy had an argument with him a few days ago."

"He never said anything about it to me."

"What about people outside the college? Social relationships?"

She looked at me for a moment, and though her face

didn't give a quiver I had that feeling again that she was going to start crying. "Women, you mean," she finally said. "Yes, that might be a good way for you to go. He was a bastard about women. Maybe he *wasn't* going to work on an article the night he was killed. After all, that's why he bought that house way out in the middle of nowhere. So he could bring his women out there, and there wouldn't be any nosy neighbors around to keep tabs on him. Yes, indeed, why don't you look into his sex life. I'll bet you'll come up with somebody he just gave the boot to—only she had enough guts to get back at him, instead of sitting still and nursing her wounds, like—like most of his snuffed-out flames would've done."

"You could supply me with some names?"

"I wouldn't think of it, even if I knew any. If it wasn't for Mike being in this terrible spot, I'd be sending her my congratulations and a bottle of champagne."

I watched her steadily. She lowered her eyes, became occupied with her glass. Then I said, "You can understand why she might've thought about killing him because you've had that thought yourself?"

She looked up at me, anger flaring in her eyes. And then, just as quickly, the flare went out, and a kind of exhaustion took its place. "Yes, I thought about it for a while. But it's all been over for a long time."

She gave a twisted little smile. "Looking back at myself then, I can't believe what I was. Naive little girl-scholar, just out of graduate school. The handsome young professor bats his sexy eyelashes at me, and I melt like a bobby-soxer, I jump into bed with him like any simpering little Victorian salivating when she hears the voice of her lord and master. And I *knew* what he was doing, too! I knew exactly the type he was! I'd read about his type a million times, my consciousness was raised, I'd seen the way bastards like him put friends of

125

mine through the wringer. But I'm not even on my own for a month when I'm letting it happen to *me*!"

"I'm sorry," I said.

She didn't seem to have heard me. "There was a kind of inevitability about it, when you get right down to it. The poor ugly overweight little girl who's terrified that no man will look at her—which will prove, of course, how hopelessly inadequate she is. Look at my bringing-up. Beverly Hills, California—the guilt center of the world! My father makes a mint as a sound technician, my mother's the champion committee-and-board member of all time. Between them they tutored me in feelings of inferiority until I became an expert. How could Stuart resist me? Can a dog resist the piece of meat that's thrown to him?"

Her smile twisted a little more. "He kept it going for two years—I should've been flattered actually, they tell me none of his other harem favorites lasted that long."

And now at last there were tears in her eyes. "Poor Stu," she said. "What was he anyway? A mechanical doll—programmed to display his charms for the opposite sex. The Seducer Doll. Because from the day he was born, that's what people told him he ought to be doing, that's what his ego was tied up in. His looks were stunning, that you have to admit. But he was as much a victim of our rotten sexist society as I am."

She broke off with a harsh laugh. "So if you want to find out who really killed him, you can do a lot better than mysterious Chicano students with earrings. Find out who his next-to-last bedmate was. Find out the name of his most recent Samantha Fletcher."

Suddenly she gave a smile, and then she began laughing. "Better still, as long as you're collecting motives, here's a terrific specimen for you—how about Marcus Van Horn? It's hard to think of anybody who would've been happier to live without Stu Bellamy."

126

"But he seems to have pushed pretty hard for Bellamy's tenure."

"What else could he do? The word came from on high. Since neither of the candidates fell into the uncomfortable category of minority—which nowadays, of course, includes women—our leaders gave Marcus a clear message that they wanted the job to go to a Member of the Club. And Marcus has the world's most sensitive radar for picking up messages from on high. But that doesn't mean he liked the guy."

"What didn't he like about him?"

"What do you suppose is the most important thing in Marcus' life, the very center and essence of his being? Not to keep you in suspense, it's the chairmanship of the department. And what do you think Stu Bellamy had his eye on, in a year or two? And made very little secret about it either. And with his connections in the administration—he played handball once a week with the dean, and the president is a distant relation of his mother—don't you think his chances of prying the treasure out of Marcus' hands were better than even? Take my word for it, Marcus was scared shitless of him."

"Would one human being really kill another human being just to go on being the chairman of a department?"

"Oh, sorry," she said. "I didn't realize we were talking about human beings. I thought we were talking about college professors."

She drained off the rest of her glass and gave a shake of her head. "Look, I've got to get home, I have a class to prepare for Monday morning."

We left The Snuggery, and I walked her to her car, which was near mine in the parking lot.

"I'm sorry I lost my cool," she said, her hand on her car door. "I'd be better off if I could take the advice of that modern poet—what's his name? Oh yes, William

Shakespeare. 'Moving others, are themselves as stone, unmoved, cold, and to temptation slow.' That was Stu's great talent, you know. It's the only thing he had that I ever envied. I told him once it would protect him for the rest of his life."

She looked startled, as if she were just that moment listening to her own words. "Seems as if I was wrong, doesn't it?"

CHAPTER 19

IT WAS SIX O'CLOCK when I got home that night. Mom had dinner heating up already, because it was Friday and she planned to go to Sabbath services at the synagogue.

At six-thirty we sat down to eat—lamb chops with a beautiful-looking mint sauce.

We talked for a while about Mom's drive to the mountains with Mr. Bernstein. "Beautiful views," Mom said. "You look out over the edge, you can see a hundred miles away. *What* you see is too small for you to recognize anything, but even so—"

"I hope Bernstein behaved himself, Mom," I said, only half joking.

"Well—" Could that possibly be a blush on Mom's cheek? "—he finally did."

A second later it was all gone, and she said, "Oh, by the way, you had a phone call, maybe an hour ago. Your boss called—Mrs. Swenson. Such a nice-sounding person. And you say she's young and attractive?"

"And happily married, Mom."

"So why not?"

"What did she call about?"

"We chatted a little to start off with. It was a big surprise to her that you've got your mother staying with you. Wouldn't it be nice if we had her and her husband the doctor over for dinner some night—"

"Mom, what did she *call* about?"

"I'm getting there, Davie. She called to tell you that she had that talk with your client Russo and it didn't do any good. He still says he won't give away his book, unless the situation becomes desperate—"

"Hold it a minute," I broke in. "Ann got pretty talkative with you, didn't she, on such short acquaintance? That's confidential information about official business."

Mom made her helpless little hand-spreading gesture. "What could I do? You know how it is—people tell me things. There's something about my face."

"Even over the phone?" But I couldn't get mad at Ann, because I certainly did know how it was. I told Mom things myself, things I shouldn't be telling anybody. I'd been doing it all my life.

So I asked Mom to go on with Ann's message.

"All she said," Mom went on, "was that she pointed out to your client, Russo, that today is Friday, and Zorro said he'd get rid of the evidence if he didn't get the book tomorrow night. She asked him how bad a situation had to become, in his opinion, before it qualified for desperation. But none of this made him change his mind."

"College professors!" I said. "They're so full of literature and philosophy that there's no room left in their heads for a little common sense!"

"You should see it from his point of view," Mom said.

"What do you mean by that, Mom?"

"He's a boy who was brought up in poverty, who found out there was only one way he could escape. With books. If it wasn't for books, he's asking himself, where would he be today? And this particular book, this poetry

130

book, for him maybe it's like a—like a—what's the word I'm trying to think of?"

"A symbol?"

"Thank you kindly. A symbol, what else? A symbol for everything he's got which, in his heart, he's afraid he could lose again overnight. He's thinking, maybe, if he lets the book go, everything else will disappear along with it."

"Mike Russo is an educated man, Mom, he's not some superstitious peasant from the shtetl."

"Is that right? You think maybe everybody in the shtetl was a dummy just because they never went to college? You think maybe people who went to college don't have down inside them somewhere their own personal superstitious peasant?"

"All right, so he's attached to his book. If he isn't careful, he'll end up reading it in the death cell!"

"Then it's our job, wouldn't you agree, to think up for him a way out?"

"Which brings us right back where we started. We thought this Vallejos kid could be a way out, but he's strictly a dead end. Because we'll never make his sister tell the truth."

"So how about making *him* tell the truth," Mom said.

"How do we do that?"

"You talk to him when his sister isn't around, you show him that you can see the hole in his story."

"*What* hole?"

"The one," Mom said, in her most patient voice, "which proves he went to see Professor Bellamy at his house on Wednesday night."

She explained it to me in detail then, point by point, and of course I was soon kicking myself because I hadn't seen it all along.

Then the front doorbell rang, and a voice called out Mom's name. The ladies from the sisterhood had come to take her to the synagogue.

131

"You're positive you won't come with me?" she said. I told her I couldn't be more positive.

"So have a nice evening," she said. "I couldn't tell you when I'll be home. Don't wait up."

After she left, I called Ann and told her about the hole in Luis Vallejos' story, and how I intended to handle him. She wanted to be in on it, too, so we arranged to meet early in the morning. Then I made some other calls, in connection with what would happen tomorrow. And then I settled down to a basketball game on TV.

The game ended at ten, but I was still awake at eleven when Mom got home.

Her face was flushed with pleasure. "We went out after Oneg to have some ice cream," she said. "A very nice group of people. And such stories they've got! Wait till I tell you the dirt about this town of yours!"

Then a look of concern and reproach appeared on her face. "Davie, Davie—you waited up!"

CHAPTER 20

EARLY SATURDAY MORNING I
parked my car half a block away from the gas station
where Luis Vallejos worked. Ann was there ahead of
me. She got out of her car and got into mine.

The station was on a busy corner a few blocks from
the college campus. It had seven or eight pumps, offer-
ing a choice of regular, unleaded, or super-leaded. I can
remember when what you got at a gas station was gas,
and you didn't have to choose a flavor.

A call to this station last night had produced the information that the Vallejos boy was supposed to be at work
at eight in the morning on Saturdays. So we waited till
seven-fifty, and then we saw him come walking down the
street. He was wearing a leather jacket and moving his
shoulders with a kind of swagger, as if to say to the
world, "I'm a big shot, don't mess with me!" We've all
seen the type plenty of times. Chicanos don't have a mo-
nopoly.

I got out of the car and stood in the boy's way.

"How are you, Luis?" I said.

He stopped short, and for a split second all that cool left him and I could see panic in his eyes. But he lowered the temperature again when he finally spoke.

"What's it about, man? I wasn't supposed to see you again!"

"Get in the car, Luis," I said. "I want you to meet Mrs. Swenson, she's my boss. She'd like to have a chat with you."

"I got no time for social conversation. I'm going to work, man."

"You've got time for *this* conversation. We have a lot of information that's going to interest you."

"I don't want to hear any of it!"

"How about the fact that we've traced the earring?" Ann said.

He looked at her, and you could see the color leaving his face.

I opened the car door. He slid into the front seat, and I sat next to him, behind the wheel. Ann was in the back seat, leaning forward.

"We found the store where you bought it," Ann said. "The salesman even remembers selling it to you."

This was pure invention on her part, but it almost fooled *me*. Outright lying is something Ann has a real talent for.

"Come on, who you bullshitting?" the boy said. "They're all the same, those earrings!"

"Not this one. There's a little nick in the glass. That's why the salesman remembers it."

"If I believed that, I'd believe anything!"

"You might also be interested to know, the DA's office called me yesterday, the lab found a fingerprint on the paperweight Bellamy was killed with. Just a smudge, somebody tried to wipe it off, but they've got a new test that brought it out."

Another outright lie. The DA's office *hadn't* called her yesterday. There is, however, a certain spy we've got planted there, and *she* had called to report that the lab in Denver hadn't been able to get an identifiable print off the murder weapon.

"Oh, yeah?" The boy's eyes were fixed intently on Ann's face. She seemed to fascinate him and horrify him at the same time. "You trying to tell me they're saying it's my print?"

"What they're saying is, it isn't Professor Russo's print and it isn't Professor Bellamy's print. It's an unidentified print, as far as the cops are concerned. But they could match it up with your finger real fast—if I happened to call you to their attention."

"You going to do that?"

"Why not? If you never had your hands on that paperweight, the print won't turn out to be yours, will it? You've got nothing to worry about." Ann moved her face a little closer to his. "But it *will* turn out to be yours, won't it, Luis? Because we know damn well you were in Bellamy's house Wednesday night."

"You can't— How do you know that?"

"You told me so yourself," I said. "When you were sounding off to me yesterday about what a racist Bellamy was. 'That big fucking collection of books he's got—hundreds of them, all the way up to the ceiling!' How could you know about those books, how could you know there were hundreds of them, how could you know they went all the way up to the ceiling? He didn't keep any of them in his office. He kept them all at his house. So when you told me you'd never been inside his house, you were lying."

· Luis moved his eyes fast to the right and left, as if he expected to find an escape hatch somewhere. "Look— it's different from what you think. I didn't waste that professor. He was a bastard, but I wouldn't kill anybody."

Ann and I didn't say anything. There are times when

the best way to get a witness to answer your questions is not to ask any.

"All right, I was out there that night," Luis said. "I didn't go back to my old man's place and talk to Flora—not till eight-thirty. She was covering up for me when she told you it was a quarter of. But when I got there, to Bellamy's house, he was dead already."

"Why did you go out there?" Ann asked.

He wet his lips, looked to the right and left again, then said, "You know how he was trying to flunk me in his course, that racist bastard. So I was mad at him, wouldn't *you* be mad at him? But the crazy thing was, I couldn't believe it. I mean, part of my mind like couldn't believe he'd go through with it. Nobody could be such a scumbag, not when the crunch came, you know what I mean? So I thought, if I could talk to him, just one more time talk to him, and maybe apologize for yelling at him—maybe he'd see reason, and maybe he'd back off like."

"You still thought he might back off, even after the things he said to you?"

"Okay, okay, it was crazy, that's what I'm telling you. I never saw anybody like him before, can I help it if I couldn't believe—" He broke off with a shake of his head. "You think I'm bullshitting you. Why not? It *sounds* like I'm bullshitting you."

"What time did you drive out to his house on Wednesday night?" Ann asked.

"It must've been around quarter of eight that I left this restaurant where I was having dinner and started out to his place. Yeah, seven forty-five on the nose. Like I told you before, I looked at the clock in the restaurant and set my watch by it. So he's on Blackhawk Road, that's out in the sticks, it took me about twenty-five minutes. Ten minutes after eight I got there."

"Did you park your car in front of his house?"

"I parked it around the corner. If he heard my car

pulling up and looked out the window and saw me coming, I thought maybe he wouldn't let me in."

"What did you do then?"

"I rang the doorbell four, five times, and nobody answered, so I figured he's out for the night."

"Even though all the lights were on?"

"Sure. A lot of people leave the lights on when they're out. They think it keeps the burglars from ripping them off."

"Why didn't you call up first, to find out if Bellamy was home?"

"Same reason I parked the car around the corner. Like I thought, if I called ahead of time, he'd tell me he wouldn't talk to me. So anyway, the bell wasn't raising anybody, so I tried the door, and it turned out it wasn't locked, so I went inside."

I couldn't stop myself from putting in a question here. "It didn't occur to you that you were trespassing?"

He looked at me with genuine puzzlement. "The door wasn't locked, was it?"

I have to admit it, sometimes I just can't connect with today's world at all. More and more people seem to have been born without any sense of privacy. They seem to think everybody has a natural right to barge in uninvited on everybody else.

"What did you do when you got inside?" Ann said.

"I was in this big fucking hallway, it's bigger than any of the bedrooms in my old man's house. And there's one of those rugs on the floor—you know, with the red and black circles on them, the kind of rugs people ride on in those Sinbad movies. And there's a table with this big vase on it. A whole table, and all it's doing there is holding up this one vase.

"So then I went through this archway like, and I'm in this room with books on all the walls, all the way up to the ceiling, I never saw so many fucking books in my life outside of the college library. Like he could've opened

137

up his own library in competition, right? And then I saw him—the professor—" Luis broke off, wetting his lips. He didn't look particularly cocky at that moment.

"He was lying on the floor?" Ann said.

"On his stomach, man. And one of his legs was kind of twisted up under him. It was weird. I never saw a dead dude before."

"What else did you notice about him? Anything odd about his clothing? Any objects on the floor?"

"Books, that's all I saw on the floor. He had them there in piles, like there wasn't room for all of them on the shelves. And the one he was holding in his hand."

"Which hand?"

"His right, I think. He was holding onto it tight, like he wasn't going to let any mother— anybody grab it away from him."

"Could you see what the book was?"

"It had these red letters. And a picture."

"A picture of what?"

"Who knows? Some dude. Big black dude. I'll tell you the truth, I wasn't looking at anything too close, you know. What I was concentrating on was trying to keep from puking on the floor. So anyway—I got down on my knees next to him—"

"Why did you do that?"

"It was crazy. I thought maybe he's still breathing. So I got down by him to find out. But I could tell he wasn't breathing. Then I saw this—I guess it's a paperweight, heavy fucking thing looks like an open book—it was on the floor next to him. I picked it up. Don't ask me why. Soon as I did it, I started thinking about the fucking fingerprints. So I wiped it off with my handkerchief and put the fucker down again. All of this—it didn't take so long. Maybe two, three minutes. Then I heard a noise, it's a car about a block away. So I decided to get the hell out of there."

"You didn't think about calling the police to report the murder?"

"I thought of it. I went up to the phone, but I didn't pick up the receiver, I left it on the hook. I mean, I was crazy, man, but I wasn't out of my *mind*. You know what the cops in this town are going to do, they find a Chicano boy inside a white man's house, bending over his dead body? And this white man just flunked this Chicano boy in a class?"

"Well, I see the point," Ann said. "Go on."

"I jumped up and ran to the door. On the way I bumped into one of those bookcases, maybe that's when my earring fell off. They're always falling off."

"You didn't get your ears pierced so they'd stay on?"

"What do you think I am, a fucking faggot? So I got out the front door, I didn't even close it behind me. And I drove like hell back to my house. And that's the truth, no bullshit anymore, man."

Ann didn't say anything more. She just looked at him.

Finally the boy broke the silence. "So—you're turning me over to the cops?"

"We'll think about it," Ann said. "Stay put. Don't go anywhere."

"I didn't kill the bastard—"

I leaned across Luis and opened the door on his side of the car. He got the hint and stepped out to the sidewalk, stared at us for a second, then started walking fast toward the gas station.

CHAPTER 21

ANN WASN'T SURE WHAT to do about this new development. Should she turn Vallejos over to the DA, or should she save him for the trial as a surprise defense witness, a hostile one, so that Wolkowicz couldn't tamper with his evidence ahead of time? She told me she wanted to sleep on it; meanwhile I shouldn't tell anyone, not even our client, about what we had discovered.

She didn't know it, of course, but by "anyone" she wasn't referring to my mother.

So I got back to the house around ten that morning, and found Mom scrubbing the kitchen floor. I pointed out to her that the cleaning woman had been in yesterday and had done that job.

"You're entitled to your opinion," Mom said.

As a matter of fact, though, she stopped scrubbing right away, because she wanted to hear about my talk with Luis Vallejos. When I told her what the boy had broken down and admitted, a big beaming smile spread over her face.

"So you really threw into him a scare? He thinks you're going to get him arrested?"

"If he doesn't think so, he wasn't paying much attention."

"Good. Wonderful. Perfect. So you know what you should do now?"

"That's exactly what Ann is trying to decide."

"Not what *she* should do, what *you* should do. At two o'clock this afternoon, in the chapel at the college, they're having a memorial service for the dead professor. I want you should go to it."

"What am I supposed to do there, Mom?"

"You're supposed to let people see you. Sit close to the front row. Say hello to everybody you know. After the service is over, hang around the chapel, talk to people. Remind them you're alive in the world. Then you should come back to the house here and wait."

"But what's all this going to lead to?"

"It's a little idea I've got, but I don't want yet to tell you."

"Not even a hint?"

"All right, you want a hint? A dark lady is going to come into your life and tell you a secret."

"Mom, it sounds like a fortune cookie!"

"Why not? You can learn a lot from fortune cookies, if you know how to read them right."

And so, at two o'clock, I was at the college chapel for the Bellamy memorial service.

I was among the last to slip in, but there was no problem finding a seat up close. There weren't more than thirty faculty and students, sitting in the central section just below the altar. The rest of that large dimly lit interior was empty. This produced a pretty eerie effect, with those imitation Gothic arches stretched high above our little group and the organ playing. No instrument gives me the creeps like an organ.

On the podium, in chairs grouped behind the college

141

chaplain, seven or eight solemn professorial types were sitting. I saw Marcus Van Horn and Samantha Fletcher but no Mike Russo.

The college chaplain is the Reverend Ethelbert Underwood, D.D., professor of religion, and I run into him every few months at dinners given by the local Rotarians, where he's called upon to deliver the invocation and the benediction. Several times I've sat at the same table with him and been entertained by his inexhaustible supply of dirty limericks.

Like so many clergymen—all creeds and denominations including all the rabbis I've ever known—Bert changes his whole personality as soon as he steps into a pulpit. His voice goes down an octave and develops a tremolo, his eyes roll heavenward, his hands clasp together, he turns into God. So it was this afternoon, as he delivered a sermon about death not being the end but the beginning. Sermon Number 10-A, they all use it sooner or later.

The professors then stood up one by one and read their poems, in historical order.

Samantha Fletcher began, in a low intense voice that kept threatening to turn into a sob, with something from the Middle Ages. It was written in some kind of Old English, which made the words totally incomprehensible.

The Shakespearean man read a sonnet by Shakespeare, all about how the deceased didn't want people to mourn for him because he loved them so much that he just couldn't bear for them to shed tears on his account.

From what I'd been hearing about Stuart Bellamy, he didn't have to worry.

Marcus Van Horn, in a voice that was reeking with sadness and solemnity—but also very controlled, so that every word carried in that big room—read a selection from Thomas Gray's "Elegy Written in a Country Churchyard."

142

> The boast of heraldry, the pomp of power,
>   And all that beauty, all that wealth e'er gave,
> Awaits alike the inevitable hour.
>   The paths of glory lead but to the grave.

Very true, I suppose. But I'll bet, in his mind, Van Horn was making an exception of full professors of English and department chairmen. *Their* paths certainly couldn't lead to the grave. God wouldn't have such a distorted sense of values.

Several other professors covered the stretch of literary history from the romantics to the moderns, and then that organ music sent us out to the campus again. After the darkness of the chapel, I blinked from the afternoon sun. After Thursday's snowstorm, we had been having nothing but bright sun. Most of the snow had melted away, you'd hardly have believed it was ever there.

On the grass just below the chapel steps, a knot of people had formed, and a line of others was filing past them. In the knot I noticed the dean of the college, Lewis Bradbury, with thick white hair whose waves must have been cultivated through hours of brushing every morning. With him were two women, one in her middle thirties, the other in her sixties, both dressed in extremely chic black dresses. The younger one was very blond, and the older one, before her hair turned white, must have been, too. Bellamy's sister and mother, I figured, all the way from Providence, Rhode Island.

I didn't join the line. Instead I wandered around among the mourners, letting myself be looked at, as Mom had told me to do. Along the way I noticed how many of them were chatting with one another very cheerfully. I've noticed that before at funerals. Sometimes, except for the costumes, it's hard to tell them from weddings.

I hung around this way for close to half an hour, until

143

the crowd in front of the chapel was down to a few stragglers. Then I went home and told Mom what I had done.

"And I'm damned if I've got the foggiest idea why I did it!"

Mom just gave me her gentlest smile. "Only wait," she said. "What time is it now? A little after four? So give it another hour. Take my word for it, you'll hear from her by five-thirty."

"Hear from *who*?"

"His girlfriend."

"*Whose* girlfriend?"

"The Chicano boy—*his* girlfriend."

"What girlfriend? He may have one, but we don't have any idea who she is."

"Of course we know who she is. It's the lady professor—what's her name?—Samantha Fletcher."

I stared at Mom for a second or two. I couldn't think of a damn thing to say.

"But you couldn't have any doubts about it, could you?" Mom went on. "When she talked to you yesterday, at that Snuggery place, you asked her if she knows any short dark-haired student who wears earrings. She said she didn't. Later on in the conversation, though, she told you don't waste your time looking for mysterious Chicano students with earrings. How did she know that the student you were asking about was a Chicano? You never mentioned that to her. She knew it because she knew the boy, he was in touch with her since you talked to him, he told her already that you were suspicious of him.

"Once I noticed this little slip, it wasn't so hard to remember something else. The boy told you that he showed his midterm exam to a friend of his, somebody who knew a lot about literature. Somebody, like the boy said, 'who knows what these English-professor dudes are looking for.' Who would be likely to know such a thing? Another student, or another English-professor dude?

144

Does it make sense this boy should think his exam deserved an A-minus just because another student told him so? Is any student going to believe, with such confidence, that some other student could be a judge of his work? But such a thing he could believe about a professor.

"So do you follow it now, why it's such a good thing you spoke tough to the boy this morning and made him think he was going to be arrested for the murder? As soon as he could, he told *her* about it, what else? And she's been worrying what to do ever since. And then she saw you at the service this afternoon, and she's been saying to herself, 'He's a kind, sympathetic type, maybe he'll listen to reason.'"

"Listen to reason about what?"

"You'll find out as soon as you talk to her. She'll phone you any minute now."

I was shaking my head. "Mom, you can't possibly make such a prediction!"

"You're right," she said. "I couldn't possibly. I'm all wrong. So suppose we sit here and wait, and if the phone wouldn't ring I'll be happy to beg your pardon."

Mom settled back in the chintz-covered rocker, folded her hands in her lap, and looked as if she was prepared to wait forever.

At that moment the phone rang, and I picked up the receiver.

"I have to talk to you—please!" said the voice at the other end of the line. "This is Samantha Fletcher from the college!"

CHAPTER 22

MOM RECOGNIZED THE VOICE, and I saw the little flash of triumph in her eyes. Along with a lot of other things in life, Mom loves her little triumphs.

I arranged to meet Samantha Fletcher in fifteen minutes, on the front steps of the courthouse. The building closes early on Saturdays, so I told her I'd have to let us in with my key, and then we could talk in my office.

I promised to come alone.

She was there ahead of me, pacing in front of the long stone steps that led up to the front entrance. She didn't say anything when I came up to her. She looked pretty shaky to me, so I took hold of her arm, and with my other hand I opened one of the small doors next to the big revolving door.

The inside of the courthouse, usually so noisy and crowded, looked like a deserted canyon. The elevators were locked, of course, so we had to climb two flights of stairs. The sound of our shoes clicking against the marble steps echoed loudly through those high-ceilinged hallways.

I opened my office door, and Samantha Fletcher slid past me quickly. As I shut the door, she muttered, "Oh God, I know I'm going to regret this! If anybody ever found out—"

"Then you'd better leave right now," I said.

She flinched, as if I had made a threatening gesture. "What do you mean?"

"I mean, if you've got information about the Bellamy murder, there may not be any way of keeping it confidential. You may have to testify in court."

She looked as if I had followed through on the threatening gesture. "But what I have to say—you won't *want* to bring it out in court. It can't help Mike—I wish it could, but it can't. All I'm trying to do is keep you from hurting somebody else."

"Luis Vallejos?"

She stared at me, then she gave a low moan. "How did you find out about us? Did Luis—?" She wasn't able to finish the sentence.

"He didn't say a word about you. He gave us a crazy story about eating alone on Wednesday night at a restaurant, he said he couldn't remember what it was called or where it was. I think he'd go off to the gas chamber without ever giving you away."

I saw that her eyes were wet, and there was a soft smile on her face. "I'd never let him do that. No matter what happens to me."

She paused, struggled to get her voice under control, then said, "I'd like to take off my coat."

It was a winter overcoat, with a faded look; I don't suppose she bought clothes for herself very often. I started over to help her with the coat, but she jerked away from me. "For God's sake, no chivalry please! I'm feeling foolish enough as it is."

I stepped back, and took the coat from her when it was off. I hung it up in the closet, as she dropped into my battered old leather armchair.

147

"Would you like some coffee?" I asked. "Or maybe something to drink?"

I keep a bottle of Scotch in the bottom drawer of my desk. I'm no big drinker myself, but sometimes it comes in handy for a client.

"No—no thank you," she said. "I want to know—are you really going to do it?"

"Do what?"

"What you and the public defender threatened to do—when you talked to Luis this morning."

"We didn't threaten anything. He was out at Bellamy's house Wednesday night, he admits it himself. We'll look into that further, and if it helps our client—"

"But Luis didn't do it. He got there too late—he wasn't *near* that house at the time of the murder. I can prove it."

"How?"

"Luis and I were together that night, just before he went out to Stu's house. He wanted to see me because he was worried about flunking Stu Bellamy's course, he wanted my advice on what to do. So we went to a restaurant, the Seafood Grotto, on Kit Carson Boulevard."

"What time was that?"

"We met there at six-thirty. The Seafood Grotto is one of our usual places. Not exactly a gourmet palace, but it's way over Luis' head in price. He never lets me pay the check, though, his manhood wouldn't stand for that. Anyway, we go there because it's very big and crowded, and the college people don't go there. Much too lower class, strictly for the rednecks.

"We take our own separate cars and meet at the entrance—too much risk we might be seen driving together. Afterward we usually go back to my place, but Wednesday night I had to put in an appearance at Marcus Van Horn's gathering, so I was planning to give Luis my house key. The idea was he'd wait for me at my house, and I'd be with him by eleven o'clock or so."

"But it didn't work out that way?"

"No. There was something funny about that night from the start. Something on Luis' mind. He even *looked* different somehow, his face was different. I know what it was now, of course, he was thinking about going out to see Stu Bellamy, about how he had to make some last attempt to get Stu off his back."

"Did Luis know about—?"

"That Stu and I were lovers once? No, I never told Luis that. He's too honest and open. Stu was riding him pretty hard in that course, and Luis could've lost control one day, and accused Stu of getting back at *me* on account of our affair. Luis could've played the noble lover standing up for my honor. And Stu was no dope, he would've figured out exactly what was going on between us. That was one thing I didn't want to happen, to give Stu Bellamy that kind of a weapon against me.

"You want me to get back to Wednesday night, don't you? Well, Luis and I had dinner, and then he went out to the men's room to comb his hair. He always does that just before we go home together. It's his little-boy vanity, I suppose. It didn't matter to *me,* I love him whether his hair is combed or mussed.

"He came back from the men's room, he looked as if he'd seen a ghost. 'I have to go,' he said, 'there's something I have to do.' He paid the check, and we left the restaurant, and he saw me to my car and said, 'I'll be at your house by ten, long before you get there. We won't lose any time at all.' Then he drove off, going very fast in that jalopy he always borrowed from his sister."

"What time was it when you and Luis left the Seafood Grotto?"

"That's the whole point, isn't it? That's why I'm talking to you now, getting ready to flush my academic career down the drain. It was about twenty to eight or so when we left the Grotto. It's only a few minutes from there to Marcus Van Horn's house, so I was at the party

149

by a quarter of. But Stu lived way out, Luis couldn't have made it from the restaurant to Blackhawk Road in less than twenty-five minutes, and that would be going fast—which I guess he was doing, because Luis likes to drive fast. The point is, he couldn't have got to Stu's house any earlier than five or ten after eight. And Stu was killed at five *before* eight—I heard it happening with my own ears."

"Can anyone confirm the time you and Luis left the restaurant?"

"Meaning a woman in love might lie to save her boyfriend's neck? Yes, I'm sure that's true. But there were people at the Seafood Grotto who must've seen us there until twenty of eight. The waitress—the woman who seats people—the people we talked to at the table next to us, all of them singing 'Happy Birthday' for this old couple. You'll talk to them, won't you? You'll see that Luis *couldn't* have done the murder!"

She stopped talking, but when I didn't say anything right away, she spoke up again. "Are you going to tell the police about him now?"

I didn't want to answer that yet. So I started a question of my own. "How did you get—" I didn't finish though, because my question already sounded pretty tactless in my ears.

"How did I ever get involved with him?" She didn't seem to be the least bit offended. "It's natural to ask, isn't it? Older women and younger men—they're still a strange sight in our society. In spite of all those ancient Hollywood glamour girls with their young studs. Though I don't see myself that way, you know. Glamorous I'm not. And not ancient either, though I'm feeling pretty close to it at the moment. And to me Luis has never been any kind of stud. I never want any man to be a stud to me. Just as I never want to be a piece of ass to any man.

"And that's not what I was to Luis either, in case

150

you're thinking it. He's a sweet boy. From the beginning that's mostly what he was, sweet. And that turned out to be exactly what I was looking for. After Stu Bellamy, I mean. Whatever else I got from Stu, sweet definitely wasn't part of it."

"How did it begin?"

"It was back in January, when Luis was just starting Stu's Nineteenth-Century American Novel class. He was having trouble with one of the books, and he went to Stu's office to ask for help. Stu wasn't there, but I was in my office, and I heard him knocking on Stu's door, and he looked so forlorn—well, I asked him if there was anything *I* could do to help, and the next thing you know he was sitting across the desk from me in my office, and I was giving him the word on Washington Irving.

"And all the time I was droning away about Ichabod Crane, I was thinking how beautiful and vulnerable and serious and—and *sweet* this boy was. Boy. I called him a boy, in my mind, that first time. I still think of him as a boy. And believe me, I *don't* think of myself as a girl. A grown woman lusting after a boy. Maternal fixation and so on. I suppose I'd had about enough of grown men for a while.

"Well, I'll try very hard to make a long story short. After that first session—that pure, high-minded, totally innocent tutoring session—I suggested it might be of some value for him if we did it again. Maybe he could come to my house some evening after dinner. Yes, it was just as crude as that. You can't blame him for accepting the invitation. For a boy of nineteen it's exciting and flattering when an older woman takes an interest in him, when for once he isn't the one who has to make the advances."

"It's been going on since the beginning of the term?"

"Two months, a little longer. It won't keep going for another two months, I can tell you that. Not that I ever expected it would."

151

"But the way he's acting now—"

"Oh yes. He thinks it's forever. He hasn't found out yet how boring it's going to be for him. One more month, that's about what I give it—if you don't drag him into this murder case." She took a breath, then went on, "You didn't answer my question yet. *Are* you going to drag him in?"

I didn't know what to say. If she was telling the truth—and there seemed to be witnesses who could confirm her story—what would be the point of bringing the Vallejos boy into the case?

But even as I asked myself this question, I could hear Ann Swenson answering it. The point would be that witnesses can be discredited when they get on the stand, people's memories are easily confused, a lot can be done just by hammering away at someone. And as for Fletcher herself—it wouldn't be hard for Ann to point out to a jury that she was an infatuated woman who might say anything to protect her boy lover. In other words, if Ann wanted to take that route, she could make it all pretty damned messy.

And if there was no other way to save her client, that would be the route she'd have to take.

"Would you really be flushing your career down the drain," I said, "if all of this came out?"

She gave one of her sarcastic grins. "The academic world moves with the times, you understand. A generation or two ago, if a professor had an affair with a student, that was enough for both of them to get kicked out on their ears. Nowadays you can get away with it as long as you're discreet and nobody talks about it. But getting it plastered all over the front page of the papers, in connection with a murder—that's going to be frowned on even in our enlightened times! And when it's a female professor and a male student who's ten years younger—"

"They can't fire you for such a thing, can they?"

"They won't *have* to fire me for such a thing. That's

the big catch in the tenure system. Once you've got it, there's almost nothing they can fire you for, but until then you're strictly on probation, you get your contract from year to year, and the school's under no obligation to renew it. All they have to do is tell you they don't want you back. They don't even have to give you a reason."

She watched me in silence a moment, then in a flat voice she said, "So I gather you're going to bring Luis into this anyway. I'll have to tell my story in court. All right, I don't blame you. You have to do your best for Mike." She sighed and raised herself to her feet. "When can I expect the roof to fall in? Will the public defender be giving a press conference, or throwing Luis to the district attorney, or what? Will it be tomorrow sometime? Morning or afternoon?"

"I don't know when it'll be," I said. "I have to talk to my boss. She has to put it up to the client." I hesitated, then I said, "Maybe we'll be able to come up with something else."

CHAPTER 23

AT AROUND SEVEN I called home from my office. Mom answered the phone and told me she was keeping my dinner hot. I said I couldn't take time for dinner just now, I'd have a cold snack later. Mom started to make one of her speeches about how I was ruining my digestion, but I cut her off by telling her about my talk with Samantha Fletcher. I could imagine her drinking in the details, carefully sorting them out in that brain of hers. She forgot all about my digestion.

The reason I had to stay downtown was that I had just told Ann about Samantha Fletcher, and Ann had decided we'd better have an emergency conference right away. And the client ought to be in on it. I was to call Mike Russo and have him meet us in her office in the courthouse.

The three of us were there in fifteen minutes. When I repeated Fletcher's story to Mike, he squeezed his hands together in his lap and gave a big sigh. "Poor Samantha. She just doesn't have a hell of a lot of luck with men, does she?"

154

"The question is," said Ann, "what are you going to do about it?"

"I don't know. Do I have any choices?"

"Only three, as far as I can see. When the trial begins I can put Luis Vallejos on the stand and make him tell his story about going out to Bellamy's house and finding the body. I can try to convince the jury that the case against *him* is a lot stronger than the case against *you*."

"But Samantha will testify that he's got an alibi."

"And I'll rip her testimony to pieces. And those other witnesses who saw her and the kid leave the Seafood Grotto—I can probably mix them up enough to plant a lot of doubts in the minds of the jury. That's one choice you've got."

"Do you know what that would do to Samantha?" Mike said. "It would be all over the newspapers that she was having an affair with a nineteen-year-old student. The college would never give her tenure, she wouldn't be hired by any college in the country. There *has* to be some other way. You mentioned a second choice—"

"The second choice," Ann said, "is Zorro."

Mike turned a little pale.

"Sure, it's a long shot," Ann said. "The whole thing could very well be some kind of stupid practical joke. On the other hand, the joker might actually have something that'll clear you and make it possible for us to leave Vallejos and Fletcher out of it."

Mike began to drum his fingers against the arm of the chair.

"He says he'll be in the park at midnight tonight," Ann went on. "Dave will be there, too, and collect whatever there is to collect—and give him the book he wants from you."

Mike's fingers stopped drumming and gripped the arm of the chair tightly. "You mentioned a third choice?"

"That's the easy one," Ann said. "No time or effort

155

required at all. Don't do a damned thing, let them haul you off to the gas chamber."

Mike's knuckles grew whiter and whiter, until suddenly he relaxed his grip and the blood flowed back into his fingers. "I'll go home and get the book," he said, in a very low voice.

I could see Ann relaxing. "All right," she said. "Wrap it up in something, brown paper maybe with a string around it. Have it ready for Dave, he'll drop by your house and pick it up on his way to the park."

Mike nodded. He was trembling, I saw. He had made the great decision, and the effort seemed to have knocked all the strength out of him. He got to his feet a little shakily, murmured "Thank you" halfway between Ann and me, and moved with care to the door.

A little later, when I got home, I told Mom I'd be going to the park again tonight. She didn't let any of her qualms show on her face. She just said, very calmly, "So what about tonight's dinner? Give me half an hour, and I guarantee it'll be as good as new."

CHAPTER 24

ON MY WAY DOWNTOWN I pulled up at Mike's house. He must have seen me coming, because he was moving down the front walk as I got out of my car. He put a book-size package in my hands; it was wrapped in brown paper and a heavy piece of cord was wound around it tightly. His fingers seemed to cling to it for a second or two before he let me take it out of his grasp. I got the feeling he'd spent a few minutes inside the house saying a tender good-bye to it, as if it were a lover he was parting from forever.

I drove on to Manitou Park. It looked darker, more deserted, more sinister, than it had looked two nights ago. The sinister part might be true, but not the deserted part. This was Saturday night: Chances were that a lot of complicated drug deals had been going on all night in those shadows. I took a quick look around, couldn't see any cops (male or female) within walking distance, and went through the gates into the park.

I headed straight for the general's elm tree in the center, carefully ignoring any suspicious shapes or noises to my right or left. I was worried that the bench next to the tree might be occupied, by somebody or other engaging in a different form of madness than myself. But the bench was empty. I sat down on it, holding my package as conspicuously as possible on my knees.

Zorro/Blood wasn't as prompt this time. I had to wait five minutes past the chiming of the hour. Finally I felt that hard hand clamping down on my shoulder.

"Glad to see you," I said.

The hand tightened on my shoulder. "Give," said that muffled voice.

I lifted the package, and the gloved hand shot out over my shoulder and pulled it away from me.

"This is supposed to be a trade," I said.

The hand let go of my shoulder. A moment later I could hear something being set down on the bench next to me. Then came hurried footsteps and that rustling noise. Old Zorro moving into the bushes behind the bench.

I looked down and saw a large rectangular package, also wrapped in brown paper and string, on the bench next to me. An envelope was fastened to the top of it with Scotch tape. Another one of those envelopes with "Mesa Grande College" printed on it.

I opened the envelope and read the note inside, written on the same kind of word processor as the first two.

Are you interested in knowing why I wanted that book? Not because I'm a collector. I can't think of anything more stupid.

I wanted it to prove a point. Russo is always saying he values that book more than his life, he'd let go of it only over his dead body. Bullshit. I always knew it was bullshit. Showing off for the gullible kiddies, like all those college professors. And it turns out I was right, doesn't it?

Now that I've shown the asshole up, he might want to know what I intend to do with his precious Emily Dickinson.

Burn it.

Best regards,
The Shadow

I put the letter in my pocket and picked up the package. It was heavier than I had expected.

I have to admit, my curiosity was almost too much for me. For a moment there I almost tore off the string and wrappings so I wouldn't have to be in suspense another minute. But my better instincts won out—also my nervousness about hanging around Manitou Park any longer than I had to. It wouldn't be fair to get a glimpse in ahead of Mom.

I lugged the package to my car. Still no sign of a cop. It was Saturday night, business was especially heavy in the park, so naturally the local patrol people were miles away.

I got back to the house, and the front door flew open before I could use my key.

"So let's see it," Mom said.

I brought it into the living room and put it on the coffee table in front of the couch. I was reaching for the string when Mom said, "Wait a second. Don't open it yet. First I'll tell you what's in it."

159

CHAPTER
25

SO WHAT WAS I supposed to say to that? The suspense was killing me, but in the fifty-three years I've known my dear mother, I've never been able to walk away from one of her challenges.

"There's no way you could tell me that, Mom," I said.

"Maybe so, but suppose I try."

She stared down at the package for a while, as if she could see through the wrapping with her X-ray vision. And then she started in, "You know what bothered me most about this murder, right from the start. It was that phone call."

"I can understand that," I said. "It *is* sort of grisly, to hear a man being killed over the phone."

"Grisly I wasn't thinking of. People murdering people is always grisly. There's no nice, pleasant way to do it. If I worried about grisly, I couldn't take an interest in murders in the first place. What's been bothering me about that phone call is, why did Stuart Bellamy make it?"

"I don't see the problem. He told Samantha Fletcher

he'd look up this quotation, to settle their argument, so when he finally found it—"

"A quotation that proved *her* point and didn't prove *his*. Fletcher and Russo, they both told you it wasn't in character for him to admit he was wrong like that.

"Another peculiar thing about that phone call. If he was going to admit he was wrong, why did he pick this particular time to do it? In the middle of a party yet! He knew there had to be people crowding and pushing around the phone, he knew the room would be noisy and a phone conversation wouldn't be easy to carry on. So why, I'm asking myself, didn't he call Fletcher at some other time, maybe at her own house when she'd be alone?

"And the things he said, the words he used—didn't they also strike you as peculiar? When you picked up the phone, Davie, and said hello, his exact words were, 'Stu Bellamy here. Samantha Fletcher, please.' He never said hello back to you, he never asked who he was talking to, he never asked if he could speak to the host, maybe to inquire from him how the party was going, maybe to express his regret for not being there. He never even said, 'Could I speak to Professor Fletcher, please?' or 'Would you kindly call Samantha Fletcher to the phone?' or some such phrase, which would have been natural under the circumstances. All he said was her name, 'Samantha Fletcher, please.' Short and quick, rude almost—and didn't Van Horn say to you that Bellamy usually had very good manners?"

"I don't see your point," I said. "He was busy writing his article, he wasn't in the mood for polite conversation."

"But *he* was the one that made the phone call. If it was such a nuisance for him to talk, why didn't he call up the next day or later? It wasn't exactly a matter that couldn't wait till his article was finished.

161

"And his conversation, when Fletcher finally came to the phone, was also a big puzzle. He was short and quick with her just like he was with you. He didn't try to make small talk. He didn't describe his state of health. He didn't apologize for pulling her away from the party. When she said who it was, he waited a couple seconds, then he jumped right in. 'All right, Samantha, you win. Here's the last paragraph of *Black Boy*.' And then he starts reading it—she interrupts, she makes comments, but he goes on reading it without paying any attention to her. And as soon as he says the last word of it, there's a bang, there's a gasp, there's a busy signal, and after that he's supposed to be dead."

"Why do you say 'supposed to,' Mom? Three people heard him reading that paragraph, and heard the blow being struck. Your own son was one of them. You don't suspect me of lying, do you?"

"If you never lied, what kind of a detective would you be? But you're right, to your mother you wouldn't lie, that I'm sure of."

"Well, there you are."

"Where am I? You're telling the truth about what you heard—but what exactly *did* you hear? You heard Bellamy's *voice* reading from that book. But did you hear *him*?"

A long pause. Then, slowly, I said, "I'm not sure I know what you mean."

"Those peculiar things I just mentioned—I can think of only one way to explain them. He didn't ask you who you were when you picked up the phone, because he couldn't be sure who *would* pick up the phone. Anybody at all could've picked it up."

"I don't follow you, Mom. Whoever picked up the phone, Bellamy would've used that person's name as soon as that person identified himself."

"But this is the point. This is exactly what Bellamy couldn't do—he couldn't carry on a conversation with somebody, even a short conversation, where he had to use the person's name."

"*Why* couldn't he?"

"Because Bellamy wasn't Bellamy at all. Like I said, it was only a voice. It was only a tape recording of Bellamy's voice."

I didn't have anything to say to that. I was letting it sink in.

"Can you have any doubts about it?" Mom went on. "Bellamy's voice was recorded earlier, and that tape was what you heard over the phone. So the voice *couldn't* ask you for your name, it *couldn't* make any small talk, it *couldn't* ask questions about the party, make apologies, talk about his illness, stop in the middle of reading the quotation to acknowledge Fletcher's comments. A live human being could do such things, but not a voice on a tape that was recorded ahead of time. Nothing could be on that tape except a quick greeting, 'Samantha Fletcher, please,' 'you win,' 'Here's the last paragraph,' and then the quotation itself."

"Wait a second, Mom. That really *was* Bellamy's voice on the phone—Fletcher and Van Horn both swear to it. So how could it be a tape recording—unless Bellamy himself was in on it?"

"Absolutely not. Why did he have to be? All somebody had to do was call up Bellamy earlier in the day and ask him, for some reason or another, to read the paragraph from *Black Boy* over the phone. *This* conversation would be taped, and afterward it would be snipped and pasted and so on—edited, is this what they call it?—with the snipper-and-paster's voice cut out and with pauses left between Bellamy's speeches. And also with sound effects at the end—bang, thud, groan, very realistic.

"This is another explanation why Bellamy sounded rude. What that other person got him to say over the phone could be snipped and pasted in plenty different

163

ways, but nothing could be *added* to it. Whoever fooled around with the tape had to use the words Bellamy actually used. So instead of saying to you, 'Could you ask Samantha to come to the phone?' the voice says, 'Samantha Fletcher, please.' Because Bellamy, in the earlier conversation, the one that was put down on tape, never said anything like 'Could you ask Samantha to come to the phone?' But he did say her name maybe, and he did use the word 'please,' and the snipper could put these two together."

"Yes, it *could* have been done that way," I said. "There's nothing against it technically."

"It's being done all the time. Haven't you had the experience lately, you answer your phone and you're listening to a recorded voice which is trying to sell you something? Such an aggravation! You can't even relieve your feelings by getting mad at the salesman!

"So the same type thing could've been done with this tape. You take a tape recorder, with the snipped-up tape in it, and you attach it with wires to a telephone. And to this you also attach a timer, like for turning your lights on and off when you don't want the burglars to know you're away for the weekend. So a second or two before seven fifty-five the timer turns on the tape recorder, the phone automatically rings at a certain number, and as soon as the person at that number picks up the receiver the voice from the tape begins to talk. I was reading last week a *Reader's Digest* at the hairdresser's, and there was an article how, in our country today, at least a hundred thousand bright high school students know how to fix up all kinds electronic contraptions a lot more complicated than this. All they need is the right equipment."

"But what was the point of going through such a rigmarole?"

"Davie, Davie, you don't see it yet? The point was for an alibi. Bellamy wasn't killed at five minutes to eight. He was killed earlier in the evening. Then the murderer came to Van Horn's house for the party and stood around in full sight of a dozen witnesses at exactly the moment—which was proved by the phone call—when Bellamy was being killed. Could any alibi be more perfect?

"And this also explains why the murderer had to pick Van Horn's party for the scene of the phone call, why Fletcher couldn't have been called up when she was alone in her own house. There had to be witnesses. More people than one had to listen to Bellamy's voice and say it was really him.

"And then there's your client, Mike Russo. The murderer's plan was not only to give himself an alibi but also to make sure Mike Russo *didn't* have an alibi. So one day last week the murderer steals Russo's keys and has duplicates made. Then, on Wednesday afternoon, he sneaks into Russo's house with a quart of mint-chip ice cream, which he knows is Russo's special favorite. He puts something in the ice cream that's going to make whoever eats it fall asleep, and he throws out any other ice cream that's in the refrigerator, so there's no chance the mint chip won't be eaten.

"Then, when Russo is fast asleep, the murderer takes his car—which he's got duplicate keys for, remember?—and drives out to Bellamy's place, maybe seven o'clock or a little later. He hits Bellamy over the head with the paperweight, he takes the phone off the hook, and he gets out of there, leaving plenty time for himself—did I also say herself?—to get to Van Horn's party before five minutes to eight. Because at five to eight the phone is going to ring, Bellamy is going to be on the line, and he's going to be killed while people are listening to his voice."

It was impressive, I couldn't get around it. "All right, Mom, let's say you're right. Who do you think was behind it?"

Mom spread her hands. "This I couldn't tell you for

165

sure. We know some things about this person though, don't we? It has to be someone with enough technical knowledge to set up the wiring and to finagle with the tape. Also, it has to be someone who owns the right-type equipment—"

"Marcus Van Horn!" I said. "He told me he's been working with tape recorders and other electronic gadgets lately, it's his hobby and he really plunges himself into it, he's even got a workroom in his basement. And he was scared of Bellamy—scared he'd take over the department chairmanship—and he obviously doesn't like Mike much either. All those snotty remarks he made about Mike's background! And his guests didn't start coming to his party till seven-thirty, so that gave him plenty of time— No, but wait a second, the call came in on Van Horn's own phone. So where did he keep this magic tape recorder, with the doctored tape on it—which had to be connected to a phone?"

"Why couldn't he keep it in his office at the college?" Mom said. "They've all got phones, those college offices. And you remember how Mike Russo described Van Horn's desk, how it looked on Tuesday the day before the murder. It was covered with all kinds of stuff, Russo said, and one of the items he mentioned was a tape recorder."

"But Mom, I interviewed Van Horn in his office on the day *after* the murder. I sat across from him at that desk, and I never saw any—" I stopped short, the light suddenly breaking. "Wait a second—it wasn't there the day after the murder, because a sneak thief got into his office and stole it! And the incriminating tape along with it!"

I turned my eyes immediately to the package in brown paper that was sitting on the coffee table. But then I gave a groan and said, "No, it won't work. Once the tape had served its purpose, Van Horn wouldn't have been crazy enough to leave it in his office, out in the open, where somebody might see it. He would've hot-footed it back to Llewellyn Hall as fast as he could on Wednesday night, to disconnect the tape recorder from the phone and get rid of the tape."

"Positively," Mom said. "But *when* could he do this? After the phone call, he had to stay in his house until the police came, and he couldn't go out again until they went away—and that was almost midnight. You're right, he rushed over to his office as soon as he could after that, but by that time he was too late. The tape and the recorder were already stolen."

"My God, these last few days Van Horn must've been frantic!" I said. "He must be waiting any minute for somebody to blackmail him with that tape!"

"*If* it's Van Horn who did it," Mom said.

Now she had me confused again. "But you just proved—"

"I proved it was somebody trying to give himself an alibi and also to put the blame on Mike Russo. All right, so Van Horn has a tape recorder which wasn't on his desk when you talked to him the day after the murder. Does that necessarily make him the murderer? Maybe it was under his desk. Maybe he took it to use at home. Was he the only person at that party, do you think, who owns a tape recorder and knows something about electronics?

"How about Samantha Fletcher, for instance? Her father is a sound technician in the movies—maybe he taught her something about it while she was growing up. And she didn't get to Van Horn's party until a quarter of eight. And she can say what she likes about how she's stopped being mad at Bellamy because he treated her so rotten, but believe me, when a woman gets treated rotten by a man, she wouldn't forget it so easy."

"Then you're saying Fletcher killed him, Mom?"

"I'm saying she's a possibility, just like Van Horn.

167

And who knows how many other possibilities we could dig up? There were plenty people at that party."

"You're right, Mom, it won't be easy to pick out the one person. But now that we've got the tape recorder, there are a lot of things I can do. I can see if it has a serial number on it. I can check stores in case somebody remembers selling it and whom they sold it to. I can find out if the person who used it left any fingerprints on it—"

"Absolutely, Davie, you can do all this if you want to. But there's one question I'd like to ask you—why should you want to?"

"Why should I want to find out who the murderer is? Doesn't that go without saying?"

"Not to me it doesn't. Your job, am I wrong about this, is to get your client out of jail. It isn't to put somebody else in his place."

"You're right, Mom. And this tape should be enough to do that job. But I'm only human, it's hard not to be curious about who made this tape."

Then I realized something, a major thing which in all my excitement had slipped my mind. "If that really *is* a tape recorder in there."

"So open it," Mom said. "Why should we have any doubts?"

I opened it, and it was a tape recorder all right, and there was one spool of tape all set up inside it. I plugged in the machine and pushed the button, and a moment later a voice, clearly recognizable, came through: "Stu Bellamy here. Samantha Fletcher, please."

I let it run longer. Richard Wright's words about the brotherhood of man rang out, and after they died away there was a loud thud, a gasp, and silence.

Mom broke it by speaking up softly. "So maybe you'd like to celebrate already? I've made a new batch of *schnecken*."

168

CHAPTER 26

THINGS HAPPENED FAST IN the next twenty-four hours.

First, I called Ann and told her what I'd been given in the park. "Good," she said calmly. "That ought to wrap it up nicely." This remark, coming from Ann, was equivalent to a gush of enthusiasm from anyone else.

Next, I called Mike. He had asked me to call him after I got back from the park, he didn't care how late it was, so I took him at his word. His reaction did my heart good. In between his questions about the tape recorder and his sudden exclamations of amazed delight—"It's really over? Everything's really going to be all right?"— he kept saying how grateful he was to Ann and me.

At the end of our conversation, Mike said he wanted to throw a party, a "coming-out" party he called it— coming out from the shadow of the gas chamber. Tomorrow night, at his house, and Ann and I had to be there: As far as he was concerned, we'd be the guests of honor.

The next day, though it was Sunday, Ann asked George Wolkowicz to see us in his office. Not room 211,

169

she insisted: his *real* office. We took the tape recorder down there, played the tape for Wolkowicz, and went through our chain of reasoning with him. We told him we expected the charges against Mike Russo to be dropped within the hour.

He didn't like it much, a spot of red was growing around his neck. He hemmed and hawed a little about how hard it might be to locate District Attorney McBride on a Sunday morning. We suggested that he tell McBride's wife it was an emergency, so she'd better drag him out of bed no matter how bad his hangover was. If we didn't get action within an hour, we said, we'd tell our story to the newspaper and the TV stations, and the district attorney's office would have a lot of egg on its face.

Wolkowicz saw the point. We left his office and went back to our own, and forty-five minutes later Wolkowicz was on the phone, telling us that Mike Russo was officially a free man. The media were being informed right now. McBride would make an official statement this afternoon, explaining how his office had worked diligently in spite of Mike Russo's arrest and had finally averted what might have been a dreadful miscarriage of justice.

It was Sunday, I could've gone back to bed until it was time for Mike's party. But I was too keyed up to sleep. The DA's office now had the tape recorder and the tape, and they'd investigate them as thoroughly as they could, but that didn't do a thing to relieve my curiosity. I decided to do a little off-hours' snooping on my own. So I started calling the stores in town where the machine might have been bought—if it *was* bought in town. If the store wasn't open, I called the owner at home. I made them all check their records for this machine's serial number, but nothing came up.

The cops would go through the same process on Monday morning, and their resources were a lot better than mine, they could put a dozen men on the job; but I had a feeling they wouldn't get any different results. That tape recorder wasn't going to be traced. Whoever killed Stuart Bellamy was going to get away with it.

At dinner that night, Mom and I talked about everything except the murder. She seemed nervous about something. She had been spending the day at one of the local hospitals, with a friend who was a volunteer there. (How the hell had Mom managed, after five days in town, to pick up so many friends?) She told me stories about the patients she had met, but her heart obviously wasn't in it. Once she even told the same story twice, which I had hardly ever heard Mom do.

After dinner I asked Mom if she'd like to come along with me to Mike's party—wasn't she curious to meet some of the characters she'd been making deductions about?—but she shook her head and said, "For me it wouldn't be much of a party."

Her tone of voice made me look at her sharply. Then she sighed and took my hand. "Come into the living room, Davie. You've still got a few minutes before you have to leave. I've got something to tell you."

"What is it, Mom? Are you feeling all right?"

"I never felt better. Sit down already. To hear this you should be seated."

"To hear *what*?"

"The truth about who did the murder."

CHAPTER 27

I TOOK THE COUCH, and Mom sat across from me in the chintz-covered rocker, which had become her favorite chair.

"What are you talking about, Mom?" I said. "You know who made that tape? You know who killed Bellamy?"

"All of that I knew last night. As a matter of fact—it's a little embarrassing to admit it—I knew a lot of things last night that I didn't say to you. Maybe I even lied to you a little."

I started to react to that, but she interrupted me by raising her hand. "*Everything* I said last night wasn't lying, you understand. Only part of it. It's true that somebody made a tape of Bellamy's voice and played it over the phone, so people would think Bellamy died at five to eight when actually he died earlier. I figured that out easy enough, because the phone call was so peculiar. But there were some other peculiar things about that phone call which last night I didn't mention.

"For instance, Bellamy's voice over the phone asked

to talk to Samantha Fletcher. So why not? He had his argument with her, he was coming up with a quotation for her, so naturally he wanted to talk to her. But why, I'm wondering to myself, didn't he also ask to talk to Mike Russo? Russo was part of the same argument, wasn't he? He was sitting on the sidelines, listening to every bit of it. And Russo, as far as Bellamy was concerned, was going to be at the party, too. So how come Bellamy didn't want to read the quotation to him just as much as to Fletcher?"

"Mom, Bellamy didn't actually want to read that quotation to *anybody*. That whole phone conversation was a fake. You proved that the murderer edited that tape—"

"Certainly, certainly. But what I'm wondering is, why didn't the murderer edit it so that Bellamy's voice asked to talk to Fletcher *and* Russo? Wouldn't this have sounded more natural and believable?"

"Maybe so, Mom. But what would've been the point of asking to talk to Mike? He wasn't even *at* the party."

Mom smiled with satisfaction. "Exactly," she said. "The voice on that tape didn't bother to ask for Mike Russo—because the person who edited that tape knew Mike Russo wouldn't be there, but forgot that Bellamy wasn't supposed to have that information. Now who could possibly know such a thing? Who could know ahead of time, for a fact, that Russo wasn't going to be in Van Horn's house at five minutes to eight?"

"I don't see where that gets us. The murderer put knockout drops in Mike's ice cream. So obviously he didn't expect Mike to be at that party."

"Expect isn't the same as being sure. How sure could anybody be that the knockout drops would actually knock Russo out? What guarantee was there that Russo wouldn't decide for a change not to eat any ice cream? In which case he'd come to the party, am I right? But that tape was made by somebody who was so sure Russo couldn't come to the phone that it never even *occurred* to him to include Russo's name in Bellamy's conversation. Somebody who knew *beyond any doubt* that Russo wouldn't be at that party. And only one somebody could possibly fit that description."

"What are you saying, that Mike made the tape himself?"

Mom just gave a little shrug.

"But that's plain crazy!" I said. "That tape was made so that the murderer could provide himself with an alibi. But it doesn't provide *Mike* with an alibi. He was at home, fast asleep, while the tape was playing. Nobody can corroborate his story—remember? As a matter of fact, he's practically the only person of Bellamy's acquaintance in Mesa Grande who *doesn't* benefit from that fake phone call."

"Naturally. This is one of the biggest pieces of evidence against him."

"Come on, Mom—"

"Listen to me already. I'll try to reconstruct it, what Mike Russo did, and then you'll understand. To begin with, he was desperate about his job. It seemed to him, if he didn't get Bellamy out of the way, his whole life would be destroyed. Because being a professor at a college was his whole life. At the same time he's no dope. He knew, with such a motive, that he'd be the biggest suspect. What he needed was an alibi. But let's face it, good alibis don't grow on trees. They're hard to finagle. And if you do finagle one, the police get suspicious, they make a very thorough investigation. If the alibi isn't legitimate, the chances are pretty good the police will find the hole in it and let out all the air.

"As a matter of fact, it's exactly like the little Greenspan girl."

"Excuse me, Mom, but who is the little Greenspan girl?"

"Mr. and Mrs. Greenspan from upstairs, when I was

174

living in the Bronx. He was a plumber, a big fat man, and his wife was big and fat, too, and the little girl, she was eleven, twelve, at the time, was taking after both of them. The mother liked chocolate peppermints, she ate up a couple boxes a week from Fanny Farmer's, but she didn't want the little girl to get at them so she hid them on the shelf at the top of her closet. The little girl found them—what else?—and then she had a problem. If she stole some of the peppermints, her mother would notice they were gone, and right away who would get the blame?

"So the little girl came up with a clever plan. She did steal some of the peppermints, and she was careful the next morning to leave the paper wrappers under her pillow. The mother got mad at her, but the little girl cried and swore she wasn't the one that did it. The mother changed the hiding place, and naturally the little girl found the new one, and again she stole some peppermints and again she left the wrappers under her pillow. This time the mother said to herself, 'She wouldn't be so dumb she'd keep leaving the peppermint wrappers under her own pillow. Somebody else is doing this and trying to put on my little darling the blame.'

"So the upshot was, the mother suspected everybody—the janitor, the next-door neighbors, the man who read the gas meter, even her husband the plumber—and the little girl went on stealing peppermints to her heart's desire, and everybody felt sorry for her because somebody was playing such a dirty trick on her."

"Now let me get this straight, Mom. You're saying Mike deliberately framed *himself*?"

"I'm saying he realized he was the one everybody would suspect first if Bellamy got killed. So he got this idea—it's a pretty smart one, I wouldn't deny it—of fixing up for himself a *reverse* alibi. Instead of *giving* himself an alibi, he decided he should take it *away* from

175

himself. He decided to fix it so there was positively no doubt about the time of the murder, and then to make sure he couldn't account for his whereabouts at that time. And along with that, he decided to arrange a fancy alibi for other people who also had motives—though not such big ones as his—for killing Bellamy.

"But this fancy alibi had to be a fake, naturally. Sooner or later it would have to be exposed—*this* was the whole point of the plan. And when it was exposed, everybody would know that the murderer tried to frame Russo, everybody would be sure he was innocent.

"So how did he go about making this happen? First of all, he was careful that everybody should know how upset and bitter he was about losing his job. He even planted in your mind, Davie, when you ran into him at the poetry show, that he was afraid he could commit a murder. Everybody's going to know he has a motive for this murder anyway, so he might as well get credit for not trying to hide it, for admitting it, for struggling to overcome it. This way people will feel sympathetic to him, they'll *want* to believe ahead of time that he isn't the guilty party.

"Next he called Bellamy up on Wednesday afternoon and talked him into reading the last paragraph of *Black Boy* over the phone. And while Bellamy was talking, his voice was being taped, and afterward Russo edited this tape. He knew how to do it from when he was a boy, working in his father's store, repairing phonographs and television sets.

"So now that he had a nice little one-way conversation between Bellamy and Samantha Fletcher on his tape, Russo took the next step. At seven-fifteen or thereabouts, he drove out to Bellamy's house—"

"Just a second, Mom. This whole scheme you're accusing Mike of couldn't have worked if Bellamy had gone to Van Horn's party along with everybody else. But Bellamy didn't let Van Horn know he wouldn't be there until an hour or two before the party began. So how the hell could Mike have known he wouldn't be there?"

"Yes, I worried about this for a while," Mom said. "Particularly when I heard from Samantha Fletcher that on Tuesday afternoon Bellamy told her and her alone, in strict confidence, that he planned to stay away from the party. But then it occurred to me, this conversation between them took place in Bellamy's office at the college around three in the afternoon—and at exactly the same time Russo was in *his* office, which is right next door to Bellamy's. Fletcher heard him using the typewriter in there, that's why she decided not to disturb him. And the walls between those offices are as thin as paper— which you found out yourself when you were searching for Bellamy's class lists.

"So like I was saying, Russo drove out to Bellamy's house at seven-fifteen on Wednesday night, and he parked his car down the street, at a snowy part of the curb so there wouldn't be any question later on which car had been parking there. It wouldn't surprise me, in fact, if Russo deliberately gave his car a flat tire on Wednesday morning, just to make sure nobody would think it was parked near Bellamy's house earlier than Wednesday night.

"So he rang Bellamy's doorbell, and when Bellamy let him in he was ready with some excuse why he was paying a call. They went into the living room, and while Bellamy's back was turned to him, Russo picked up the paperweight from the desk and hit him. Then he took Bellamy's phone off the hook and went home quick. Then he dialed Van Horn's number, and played the edited tape through the phone to Van Horn and Samantha Fletcher and also, as it happened, to you."

"I can see another problem, Mom," I broke in. "How could Mike be sure, when he edited that tape with Bellamy's voice on it, that it would take just exactly a certain amount of time for me, or whoever else picked up the receiver, to bring Fletcher to the phone? How could he possibly time the pause on the tape? The person who answered the phone might've taken too long to find Fletcher, and in that case Bellamy's voice would've started in talking to nobody at all. Or this person might've found Fletcher right away, and in that case she would've said hello into the phone long before the voice was ready to answer her. Either way, the whole plot would've blown up."

"Who says so? Your argument would make sense if the tape-recording trick had actually been what Russo wanted everybody to believe it was. If the tape, that is, had been playing in an empty room somewhere, while the maker of the tape, the murderer, had been in Van Horn's house, establishing his alibi. But with *this* scheme the tape didn't have to unwind itself in an empty room. Russo could be right there in the room with it, listening on his own phone in his own house to what was being said at the other end of the line. And tape recorders are equipped, isn't it so, with 'pause' buttons? So as soon as Van Horn went off to fetch Fletcher, Russo pushed the 'pause' button, and he let go of it again only when he heard her voice on the line.

"As it is, incidentally, he didn't let go of it soon enough. You told me yourself there was a hesitation— for a few seconds, and for no particular reason—between the moment when Fletcher said hello into the phone and the moment when Bellamy started in to tell her about the paragraph from Richard Wright. What could account for that hesitation, except that Russo wasn't quick enough on the uptake when he had to release the 'pause' button?

"So the guests at the party, including Van Horn and Fletcher, had their alibis now, and Russo didn't. A very touchy situation for him—he was pretty sure the police would arrest him. But it wasn't his intention he should stay arrested for long. This is what Zorro was for. And Captain Blood. And The Shadow."

"That was *Mike*?"

"Who else? It was necessary for his plan that he should find some way to get that edited tape and that tape recorder into the hands of the public defender and the police. Because the tape was conclusive evidence that he was an innocent man and that somebody was trying to frame the murder on him while they set up an alibi for themselves. So he made up a fictional character, this student who makes money on the side by being a sneak thief. He wrote a letter in this character's style, he sent it to his own lawyer's investigator—"

"You're saying there *was* no sneak thief? The tape recorder was never stolen from anybody's office in Llewellyn Hall?"

"Exactly. This was strictly part of the story he had to make up—"

"But Mom, Van Horn *did* have a tape recorder stolen from his desk. I can swear it wasn't there when I interviewed Van Horn the day after the murder. The desk was a mess, but even so I can swear there was nothing on it but books and papers."

"Who says it was there *before* the murder?"

"Of course it was. Mike described the things on Van Horn's desk—" I gulped and couldn't finish the sentence.

"So it all comes down to Russo's word, isn't that right?" Mom said. "If he didn't mention it, how would we know Van Horn ever *had* a tape recorder in his office? As a matter of fact, didn't Van Horn tell you he does his research and *dictates* his notes at home? Which means that's where he keeps his tape recorder.

"So let's get back to Zorro. What a fancy plot Russo cooked up! Zorro makes a phone call to you in a low hoarse voice, like he's got cloth over his mouth. He

179

sends you mysterious letters with crazy signatures. He gives you this exciting story about stealing the important evidence and trading it for Russo's rare book. It's better than a television cops-and-robbers show. Though naturally he does all this with a minimum amount of talking to you, because even with his voice disguised you might recognize it.

"And then, when you report to Russo about Zorro's proposition—what a performance he puts on for you! He's in such an upset state, the book is his most precious possession, he *can't* give it up even if he has to risk his life. And then, bit by bit, while all the other possibilities for saving him are going out the window, he's forced to change his mind. Finally, for such an unselfish reason— he doesn't want Samantha Fletcher's career to be destroyed—he agrees you should trade the book for Zorro's evidence. And everybody is in tears from such self-sacrifice.

"Only Russo is laughing up both his sleeves—because at a quarter to twelve you took the book from him, and twenty minutes later, without knowing it, you gave the book right back to him. In other words, he never lost his precious possession at all. It was strictly a smoke screen, which he put up to make everybody believe in a miracle: the sudden appearance of the evidence that's going to save his neck."

"But why did this scheme have to be so complicated, Mom? If all he wanted was to get the tape recorder into our hands, why not just send it to Ann and me, with an anonymous note? Why all this hocus-pocus with the park and the book?"

"My guess is he had three reasons. First, if the tape recorder just arrived one day in your mail, this would look too easy, too convenient. You'd be more likely to smell a rat. You had to think you were really *working* to get hold of that evidence. Second, he wanted to build up for you a very definite picture of Zorro's character and personality—the wild happy-go-lucky student, the child-ish nut who gives himself names from movies and comic books, the joker who's also got a nasty streak in him and wants to take poor Professor Russo's book away from him out of pure malice. To make you believe in this pic-ture, he had to go through the hocus-pocus.

"And third. I think maybe he *enjoyed* the hocus-pocus. It's not such an exciting life being an English pro-fessor in a town like this—especially if you grew up in New York. It's a nice life, and he likes it, but sometimes maybe it gets just a little bit boring. Playing kiddie games, throwing up smoke screens, being Zorro and Captain Blood and The Shadow—it's one way to kill the boredom.

"And he did a good job at it, we have to give him credit. In fact, there were only two little problems that he didn't plan for ahead of time. The first one was, the assistant district attorney decided, after he was arrested, that he shouldn't be released on bail. What a terrible blow *this* must've been to Russo! If he was locked up until he went on trial, how could he get at that tape re-corder, how could he arrange it so the tape was delivered to the public defender? No wonder he turned pale and his voice shook when he told you how much he hated being in jail. But this part of the story had a happy end-ing for him. The judge let him loose, he could go on with the rest of his scheme.

"The second unexpected problem that came up wasn't nearly so important. Did you notice how, for your first appointment with Zorro, he was right on time, on the stroke of midnight, but for your second appointment he was five minutes late? Why? He's so anxious to get his hands on that book, and still he's late? The answer is, he couldn't help himself. You made it necessary he should be late, Davie, when you told him you'd stop by his house to get the poetry book from him just before you went to the park to meet Zorro. This meant, naturally, that he couldn't leave for the park until after you did.

"Mostly, though, his Zorro scheme worked fine. We all fell right into the trap. Me, too, for a while. I can hear myself giving out with the brilliant psychology, how the book was a symbol in Russo's mind for the way he escaped from his childhood poverty! I'm a little ashamed of myself, I wouldn't deny it. But luckily, I stopped making with the psychology and started using my brains, and I saw the mistakes he made."

Mom sat back in her chair. The lecture was over, and I wish I could say it left me cool and collected. But I was more than confused and upset; I was good and mad, positively boiling. I kept thinking about Mike Russo, my young friend, my fellow bagel lover, laughing up his sleeve—up *both* sleeves, as Mom said—while he made a damned fool out of me. All right, I wasn't only mad—underneath I was hurt.

And another thing I have to confess—I was just a bit annoyed with Mom, too.

"One thing I don't understand," I said to her finally. "Why didn't you tell me all of this last night, when we unwrapped the tape recorder? Why did you let Ann and me go to Wolkowicz today and arrange for the charges against Mike to be dropped?"

"I'm sorry, Davie," Mom said. "Believe me, hiding things from you doesn't give me any pleasure. But it was necessary so that justice can be done."

"How do you figure that one, Mom?"

"Suppose I told you all this last night, what could you do with the information? You'd tell all about it to your boss, that nice Mrs. Swenson, and the two of you would have to keep it quiet. Because you're officially defending Russo, and everything a lawyer finds out about his client, if it's connected with the case, has to be kept confidential. So it wouldn't matter what you knew, it would still be your legal duty to bring that tape to the district attorney and use it to get Russo free. And you couldn't come out with the truth about him *afterward,* because you learned that truth while he was still your client. This is the law, isn't it, or am I wrong?"

I was beginning to see her point, and my annoyance was easing up fast. "Yes, that's the law all right."

"On the other hand, look what's happening because I *didn't* tell you everything last night. You forced the district attorney to drop the charges, the case is over—and Mrs. Swenson isn't Russo's lawyer anymore. So anything you find out about him *now,* it's strictly legitimate for you to tell the police about it."

"You know, you're absolutely right about that, Mom. I guess you *had* to keep a few things from me last night. Please don't make it a habit though."

"Believe me, Davie, such a thing couldn't happen." She leaned forward a little. "So what now? You'll call up the district attorney, and you'll tell him how Russo is the guilty party after all?"

I smiled at this, feeling just a bit superior. An unusual feeling when I'm dealing with Mom, and therefore, I admit, rather gratifying. "You're pretty good at *discovering* killers," I told her, "but I think I've got a little more experience than you when it comes to catching them and getting them convicted."

"I don't follow you, darling."

"What you've figured out about Mike Russo sounds dead right to me, Mom, but it's still strictly a theory. We don't have any *evidence* yet, at least not the kind that would stand up in court."

"The police will trace the tape recorder—"

"I tried that already—all day today I tried it, and I couldn't do it. Do you think I've got more confidence in Marvin McBride's efficiency than I do in my own? Believe me, if I go to the police with your theory, they won't do a thing. They'll laugh in my face. And Mike will get away with murder."

"Then what do you think you should do?"

"Catch him off guard. Throw a scare into him. Trick him into admitting what he did."

"But how are you expecting you should do all this?"

"It's simple. When I go to Mike's party tonight—"

"Davie, you're not planning on going to that party! Knowing what you know about this fellow—"

"I've got no choice. I'll wait around till after the party is over, till Mike and I are alone in his house. And then I'll tell him everything you just told me. With a little luck, the shock will make him break down and confess what he did—and somewhere in his story will be some facts that the cops can build a case on."

"If it doesn't work—"

"Then the situation won't be any worse than it is right now. This is the best chance, believe me, Mom. If you think it's important for justice to be done."

She shook her head, a worried look on her face. "You'll be alone in his house with him. And he already killed somebody once."

"I'll tell him I've explained my theory to Ann Swenson and a lot of other people. He'll realize it wouldn't do him any good to kill me, it wouldn't be logical."

"Providing he's in the mood to think logically!"

I laughed and put my arm around her shoulder. "It'll be all right. After all, it's—"

"It's your job. Thank you very much, I heard that one before."

Then she sighed and patted me on the cheek and told me to go off to my party since I obviously had my mind made up to do it. But where I got my stubbornness from she'd never be able to figure out.

At nine o'clock I said good-bye to her. It did occur to me that her manner was strangely calm and untroubled. In fact, she had made a positively miraculous recovery from her earlier mood of anxiety. But there wasn't any time to give this mystery much thought.

CHAPTER 28

MIKE LIVED IN A middle-grade neighborhood not too different from my own. His house, which I had never actually been in before, had the same New Englandy outside as mine, but it was about half the size and there was only one floor to it. It looked clean and painted, and there was no junk on the lawn or the front porch.

His living room, which wasn't very big, was crowded with people. They overflowed into the kitchen and the hall, and their coats were piled up in an adjoining bedroom. You couldn't see the big double bed for coats. There was a table in a small dining room located between the living room and the kitchen, and this table was spread with bottles, everything from whiskey to wine to imported Dutch beer, and with trays of hefty meat sandwiches.

Mike came up to me, and I saw that he had Ann in tow, too. He took us each by the arm and led us around the room to introduce us to people. He called her "Perry Mason" and me "Sam Spade," and sounded off to everybody about how the welfare of the downtrodden in Mesa Grande couldn't be in better hands than ours. His face had a flush on it, his eyes were bright, he did a lot of laughing, even when there wasn't anything in particular to laugh at.

He finally let Ann and me enjoy our drinks and food without being pulled in a dozen directions at the same time. She looked as if she were suffering intensely. She kept glancing at her watch. "Joe's in surgery tonight," she said, "but he ought to be home by ten. I want to be there when he gets in."

As good an excuse as any to duck out early, I thought.

But I couldn't use an excuse, I had promised Mom I would stick it out to the bitter end and after. So I took a seat on the couch and noticed for the first time that the room was filled with music. Harsh pounding screeching music that came from two large stereo speakers in the corners. I thought I recognized it, but when Mike came within reach again I asked him what it was.

He confirmed that it was the Bartok Sonata for Two Pianos and Percussion. It's a piece I'm crazy about myself, as a matter of fact, though I don't let too many people know about my fondness for classical music. They look at you as if you're some kind of dinosaur. Classical music isn't big in the Mesa Grande courthouse world.

I turned my attention to the guests. And they were quite an assortment. I recognized seven or eight people from the English department. There was Samantha Fletcher gulping a glass of beer, deep in argument with a pudgy dough-faced young man whose whole personality seemed to be concentrated in his horn-rimmed spectacles. There was Marcus Van Horn, fondling a wineglass between his fingers, smiling and purring at Lewis Bradbury, the white-haired dean.

"Yes, indeed," I overheard Van Horn saying, "the discovery of that tape recording does cast a certain aura of suspicion over those of us who attended my party last

186

Wednesday night. Especially over the English department, since most of us *were* English professors. Regrettable, truly regrettable. But no, Lewis, since you ask me, I *don't* think it's going to have a discouraging effect on enrollments in English courses. As a matter of fact, I've received half a dozen calls this afternoon from sophomores who have suddenly decided to become English majors—and school isn't even in session today!"

In another corner of the room was Bert Underwood, the college chaplain, coaxing cascades of giggling out of a trio of female students. I caught just a few words of what he was saying:

> There was a young woman from China
> Who was born with an extra vagina . . .

The voices around me got louder and louder, the smoke was thick enough to make me cough. The Bartok ended, and somebody put on some rock music. The din made the ashtrays rattle, and made my teeth rattle, too. I wasn't the oldest person in that house, but I felt as if I was at least a hundred and ten. God, how I wished I could go home!

But I gritted my teeth and suffered until the exodus finally took place. And oddly enough, this wasn't particularly late, not even eleven o'clock. The party hadn't really been a good one. Everyone was jubilant because of Mike's miraculous deliverance, but somehow the jubilation never seemed to get off the ground. I wondered if somewhere, deep inside all these well-wishing friends, was some small semiconscious inkling of the truth.

Probably not. It was only me. I had the sour taste of that truth in my mouth.

So I waited around till the last cluster of guests went pushing out the front door, yelling their congratulations over their shoulders. It was a little embarrassing, to tell you the truth. I've never been the type that holds on to the dregs of a party for dear life, as if I was afraid of facing myself alone in my bathroom mirror.

As the last car careened off into the darkness, Mike turned back into the living room where I was sitting on his couch. He gave me a funny look. He was asking himself why the hell I didn't have the good grace to go home with everybody else, but he was too polite to say this out loud. With his strict Italian mother, Mike was really a very well-brought-up young man.

"So—Dave. Pretty good party, wasn't it? I'm glad you don't have to run off. You want another drink?"

I told him I had drunk my quota.

"So have I, if you want to know. When the evening started, I was positive my capacity was infinite. No limits to the appetite of a man who's just been pulled from the jaws of death!" He laughed, then sighed. "But it turned out my capacity is the same puny thing it was before all this happened. Tell you what. What I *really* feel like is a cup of coffee. How'd you like to join me?"

I didn't much want him to serve me his coffee, here in his house. But I couldn't think of any way to turn him down.

"It'll only take a few minutes," he said. "It's all made already. What do you take, cream or sugar or both?"

I told him I took neither. Strong and black and bitter would suit me fine.

As he moved out to his kitchen, he flipped a switch somewhere, and the music swelled out of his stereo speakers again. It was Tchaikovsky this time, the opening of Swan Lake—that long dark throbbing theme that lets you know that everybody on stage is doomed.

He returned from the kitchen a few minutes later with two steaming cups on a tray. "I've got this new contraption," he said, "it heats up the coffee in practically no time at all. It's amazing what they can do with technology nowadays. I *love* new contraptions. If I had the money, I'd buy every different kind of invention that's on the market."

We sipped in silence for awhile, letting Tchaikovsky flow around us.

"Take this stereo of mine," he finally said. "The latest equipment, every component is the best on the market. Well, the best I can afford. Terrific sound, isn't it? I tape this stuff myself, right off public radio. It's crazy, when you get right down to it. Ten years ago my equipment wasn't nearly as good, I wasn't getting anything close to this kind of fidelity and depth. But I was perfectly happy, in fact I was convinced nothing could sound better. Today, if I still had those old components, they'd drive me out of my mind."

"You're a product of the age," I said.

"Well, we all are, more or less, aren't we?" he said. "Maybe I just don't fight against it as much as some. Or *pretend* to fight against it, like a lot of my fellow academics."

He laughed, took another sip of coffee, and silence pressed down on us again.

"It's a very nice house you've got here," I finally said.

"Glad you like it. As a matter of fact, it means a lot to me. I never had a house of my own till I came out here and bought this one. My homes were always shared with people. The place in the Bronx where I grew up, it seemed crowded with only Mama and Papa and me. And the dorms at college—always someone ahead of you in the bathroom. And those ramshackle grad-school boardinghouses."

"Actually I've never been in one of those."

"What I hated most about them was the noise," he said. "You couldn't shut any of it out. You had to live in the middle of other people's laughing, fighting, snoring, belching. Yes, and fucking. Three years ago, when I put down the first payment on this house, I felt as if my exis-

189

tence as an independent human being was just beginning. I was twenty-six, and I was walking on my own feet, without a cane, for the first time in my life. That could be why I don't want to get married. I'm still getting too much of a kick out of standing on my own feet."

He stopped talking and ran his hand through his dark, permanently unruly hair. After a moment, he said, "Well—tomorrow's Monday, you know—I've been away from my class over a week now—" He paused, with an apologetic but definitely suggestive look on his face.

"Sure, you have to get to bed," I said. "So do I, as a matter of fact. The only reason I've been hanging around so late—I thought it was only fair to tell you about it first."

"Tell me what?"

"The truth."

He lifted his cup to his mouth, and gave me a smile over the rim. "The truth about what?"

"Stuart Bellamy's death."

His smile didn't waver a bit. "What do you mean, you're going to tell me about it *first*?"

"Before I tell anybody else. The people who have to know."

His smile grew a bit puzzled. "I don't get it, Dave. Is this some kind of a riddle or something?"

A wave of tiredness came over me, but I shook it off. "I probably ought to explain," I said.

And so I explained, and when I was finished, Mike lifted his hand and covered his eyes.

"You'll never understand," he said. "In a million years I could never make you understand."

"Why don't you try me?"

"I'll never even make you believe me. Everything you've just been saying to me—it's all true. I did all those things. Except one. I didn't kill Stu Bellamy."

CHAPTER 29

AFTER A MOMENT, I said, "Come on out with it, Mike. From the beginning."

At this he uncovered his eyes. "The beginning!" A sardonic smile twitched at his lips. "They're the ones who began it. That's what you have to see. They pushed me into planning murder. If it wasn't for them, I never even would've thought about it."

"Who do you mean by 'they'?"

"They! They! Marcus Van Horn, Dean Bradbury, Stu Bellamy—all those cozy, genteel, self-satisfied WASPS with their cultured voices and superior expressions—sitting in their beautifully furnished houses and screwing nobodies like me!"

"How can you blame *them* for what *you* did?"

"Because I'm not the kind of person who kills people. Violence of any kind revolts me. It horrifies me. I've never even liked it in the movies. But they fixed it so I didn't have any other choice. Like a cornered rat. You know what cornered rats do!"

"You're talking about your tenure decision?"

"Damn right that's what I'm talking about! Sitting there in Van Horn's office last Tuesday—my God, was it less than a week ago? It seems like another existence! Listening to that genteel cultured purr of his—how kind, how sympathetic, what delicacy and finesse while he fastens his claws in my neck!

"And you know what he kept saying to me? 'Nobody could be sorrier about this than me,' he kept saying. What the hell was I supposed to do? Commiserate with *him* because *my* life was being destroyed?

"I remembered where I came from then, who I really am. Sure, I love the academic world, the intelligent cultivated people, the talk about books and ideas, the students looking up at you while they soak in your words. But with me that world isn't bred into the bone, it isn't where I was born, it isn't how I grew up. I didn't start off in some cozy Anglophiliac cocoon, like Van Horn and his kind. Where I came from you had to be tough. So I've been telling myself this last week—to protect what I've earned, what I'm entitled to, I'm willing to be tough again."

"Violence doesn't revolt you so much after all?"

"It does! It makes me sick. Do you think I *wanted* to go back to what I used to be? I've spent my whole life getting away from all that. But what could I do? Sometimes you have to do things that make you sick. In self-defense. People have a right to defend themselves."

"By killing somebody else?"

"That's what war is, isn't it? Stu Bellamy was like—like an enemy in battle. It was him or me. It's just one of those things, neither of you are to blame. Do you know what C. S. Lewis says about that somewhere?"

"No, I don't."

"He writes about two soldiers who kill each other in battle. Then the last trumpet sounds, and they rise from their graves together, they greet each other warmly like old friends, they march off to heaven arm in arm.

"That could be me and Stu, don't you see? Arm in arm. Even though we never liked each other much when he was alive. But afterward—when the last trumpet sounds—we wouldn't be each other's victims anymore. We'd both understand that we were victims of something bigger, the powers that make innocent people like us kill each other in war."

"Is the principle the same," I said, "if only one of the soldiers gets killed—and the other one takes his job?"

He shook his head in confusion. "You're missing the point—"

"So you decided Bellamy had to die. What did you do after that?"

"I knew that I'd be needing an alibi. Nobody had a stronger motive to kill him, the police would pick me up in no time flat, unless I had an absolutely airtight alibi. For a while I couldn't think of how to work it. And then, on Tuesday afternoon, when I was in my office, I heard Stu telling Samantha he was going to stay home the next night, not go to Van Horn's party. And that's when I got the idea.

"It wasn't very hard to do at all. I knew I couldn't use my own tape machine, because people may have seen it and noticed it in this house. But I've got a second one, an old one that I bought in New York years ago—nobody's ever going to trace it to me. Then I had to make the tape.

"I called Stu up Wednesday afternoon and turned on the recorder while we spoke. I told him I was doing a paper for some conference next month—I invented the damn conference—and I wanted to bring in that passage from Richard Wright's *Black Boy,* and I needed his help because I didn't have a copy of the book. I nearly fouled up the whole damn thing when I said that."

"How so?"

"He got suspicious as hell for a few minutes. You have to understand about academics. Stu has been doing a lot

193

of stuff lately about American black writers. He couldn't care less about them, if you ask me—what he really thought about blacks was, they should go back to the slave quarters where they came from—but blacks are in these days, and Stu was carving out a nice little niche for himself: the white upper-class professor who isn't too proud to get his hands dirty in lower-class minority literature. In other words, Richard Wright was his property, the live game he'd marked out for himself, and he didn't much like the idea of some pushy little wop poaching on his preserves.

"I had to do a lot of fast talking to keep him from hanging up on me then and there. I told him I wasn't really planning to deal with Wright at all in my paper. My paper was about Walt Whitman's ambivalent attitudes toward slavery, and I just wanted to use the Wright book for a couple of unimportant footnotes. What's more, I'd make sure to give credit to the wonderful articles *he* had done on Wright's work. Well, that calmed him down. He liked the idea of his name being read out to all those academic big shots. That's fame for people like Stu and me—how many footnotes you can muscle your way into."

"So he got the book and read you the passage over the phone?"

"Right. And then, as soon as he was off the phone, I started editing the tape with our conversation on it. I've got an editing attachment, I use it all the time with my own tape machine, it didn't take me too long. And it was kind of an interesting problem, too, like a jigsaw puzzle. Taking my own voice out, and rearranging his words, and putting in the pauses. Then I set it up on my machine, and had myself a drink, and at a quarter of seven I started driving out to Stu's house."

"Did you know what you were going to do when you got there?"

"Sure I knew. I was going to give him some excuse for

my dropping in—maybe I'd tell him I was hoping to borrow *Black Boy* from him for a few days, so I could find some other beautiful passages in it—something like that. Then, as soon as he turned his back to get that book off his shelf, I was going to hit him over the head, hard enough to kill him. I figured I could bring it off, even though he was bigger than me. I'd have the advantage of surprise, and I'm stronger than I look. And I took a weapon with me, a wrench from my tool chest, I put it in the pocket of my overcoat. It's a big heavy thing, but it fits neatly into my hand, and they design them so they'll be easy to manipulate."

"All right, what happened when you got to his house?"

"I parked my car down the block, next to a vacant lot. You're right, I was careful to pick a spot with a lot of nice wet mud in it. I wanted my new tire to show up clearly for the cops. Yes, you were right about that one, too—I did puncture my own tire, so I'd be sure to have a brand-new one that I couldn't have put on before that afternoon. Actually, Dave, it was pretty smart of you to see that.

"Then I went up the porch, and I saw the front door was halfway open. I knocked on it and called out, but I didn't get any answer. I knew he was there, I'd talked to him only a couple of hours earlier, and besides all the lights were on in the house. I figured he was at his desk, typing or something, so he didn't hear my voice. And by accident he'd left his door open. He should've been more careful, a burglar could've got in. But that was Stu. He didn't believe any burglar would have the nerve to break into his royal palace.

"So I went into the hallway, still calling out his name. Then I thought I heard noises from the living room. I went in there, and—" He hesitated, his voice suddenly losing power. But a moment later he forced himself to go on. "He was lying there on the floor. He wasn't dead.

195

He was making these noises. Not words, kind of—gurgling noises. Somebody got there ahead of me—a burglar, maybe—he shouldn't have kept that front door open."

"Was he lying on his back or on his stomach?"

"Face down. One leg twisted under him."

"What about the paperweight, the open book?"

"It was on the floor next to him. A foot or two away from his head. Bloody as hell." Mike jumped to his feet suddenly. "Don't you see, Dave, that *proves* I didn't do it! Why would I hit him with that paperweight when I had a wrench in my pocket?"

If you had it in your pocket, I thought, but this wasn't what I said out loud. "So what did you do?"

"I got on my knees by him. Those gurgling noises were still coming out of him. He was moving his lips a little. I said, 'Stu, what happened?' He didn't answer. His lips stopped moving, and the gurgling stopped, too. He was dead. He died right there, while I was kneeling down beside him."

He paused, seemed to see something in my face, and went on in a higher voice, "You don't believe me."

"If you're telling the truth, if you just found his body there, how come you didn't call the cops?"

"How could I? I knew nobody would believe me. I knew it right then, while I was kneeling next to him. I had the motive, I had the opportunity. What's more, if I called the police, they'd search my house before I could get rid of that tape of Stu's voice. The whole damn situation was so frustrating—like one of those nightmares where you're running and running but you can't seem to get anywhere. I was royally screwed, and I did it to myself. I could've sat tight and made no move at all, and Stu would've been killed anyway, and I would've got my tenure—and I wouldn't have a single thing on my conscience!

"Well, that was when I decided what I had to do. The

only thing I could do. I couldn't call the police. I couldn't hotfoot it right out of there and drive back to Van Horn's house, because I'd still be the chief suspect, on account of my motive, and a whole crowd of people would testify that I didn't get to Van Horn's until eight or a little before, which would make it highly possible I killed Stu before I arrived. In other words, the very thing would happen to me I'd been trying to avoid with all my fancy preparations.

"So it seemed obvious to me at that point, I couldn't afford to let those preparations go to waste. Even though I hadn't killed him, I needed to work that reverse-alibi gimmick just as if I *had*. I'd have to go through exactly the same routine I'd been planning to go through before.

"The first step was to find a copy of *Black Boy* on Stu's bookshelf. Everybody would have to think he was killed while he was reading it over the phone, so when I found it I put it into his right hand and closed his fingers down on it tight." He paused, shutting his eyes briefly, then opening them.

"You weren't afraid of leaving fingerprints?" I said.

"I was wearing gloves, of course. I did go there to kill him, do you think I wouldn't take such a simple precaution?" For a moment there was a glint of offended pride in his eyes. Then he went on, "Well, as soon as the book was planted there, I took the telephone off his desk and put it on the floor near the body. Then I took the receiver off the hook, so it would look as if Stu had been talking on the phone when he was killed.

"Then I got out of the house pretty damn quick, slamming the front door behind me."

"What time was that?"

"Seven twenty-three exactly. I looked at my watch. I hadn't been in his house more than eight minutes—I could hardly believe it.

"Well, I went back to my car, and when I opened the door I saw by the light there was blood on the sleeve of my overcoat and on my gloves. I drove back here as fast as I could—but not so fast I'd be picked up for speeding—and as soon as I got here I dialed Marcus' number. That was around five to eight. When he answered I turned on the tape recorder, putting it right up against the mouthpiece of the phone—well, you know about all that. Then I left my house for the second time that night and drove over to the party. I knew the cops would be there by then, I pretended to be surprised."

"What did you do about the bloodstains on your coat and gloves?"

"When I got back from Stu's house, I started them soaking in hot water in the bathtub. Later that night, three or four hours later, they were clean again, so I put the coat back in the hall closet and the gloves in my dresser drawer."

I felt a small twinge of satisfaction, which I carefully concealed. The incriminating fact I'd been waiting for, the fact that the DA could build a case on, had finally dropped into my lap.

"And the next day, when you got out on bail," I said, "you sent me that anonymous note?"

"That's right. And I met you in the park that night, and gave you my A-number-one imitation of Deep Throat. It was kind of fun, to tell the truth—" He broke off, and the next moment his face seemed to crumble. "What are you going to do?" he said.

I looked at him for a while. Then I said, "What *can* I do? I'm an officer of the court. If I find evidence that somebody committed a murder, I have to turn it over to the DA."

"But I *didn't* commit a murder!"

I said nothing to that.

"Your boss is my lawyer," he said. "You're her representative. Everything I told you is confidential, it's against the law for you to tell anybody about it."

"The DA dropped the charges against you this morning," I said. "Ann isn't your lawyer anymore."

"But, Dave, for God's sake, what *good* would it do to tell people about me? You don't have any evidence, nothing that'll stand up in court. I cleaned the blood off my coat and gloves, there are no witnesses to testify against me."

"You shouldn't have told me about the coat and gloves, Mike," I said. "It isn't as easy as people think to wash all traces of blood from a garment. They've got tests nowadays that can bring out latent bloodstains even after a few years. And it wouldn't do you any good to get rid of those things. People have seen you wearing them, questions could be asked about where they are. And anyway, it's no cinch making a coat or even a pair of gloves disappear. Garbage dumps can be searched. Things that get thrown in the river have a way of coming to the surface. And cloth, especially thick cloth, takes an amazingly long time to burn. In fact, it hardly ever burns completely, some of it is always left for the lab to work on. The jury might very well think it was enough to convict you—"

"The jury! My God, if there was a trial—don't you understand what that would mean? Even if they *didn't* convict me—just the fact that I went to trial would kill my chances of getting tenure! People who don't have tenure yet—the college can fire them whenever it wants without even giving a reason."

"Yes," I said, "I've heard that."

"I'll never get another teaching job," he said. "Why do you think I went through all this in the first place? I did it so I could go on teaching! My God, without that it's all over for me anyway!"

I didn't say anything.

"And I didn't kill him! That's the crazy part of it—I didn't even kill him!"

199

"Let's suppose I believed that," I said. "I don't see how it changes things much. You *planned* to kill him, didn't you? You went to his house with a weapon in your pocket. You *would* have killed him if you hadn't found him dead already. A lot of people would say you're just as guilty as if you *had* killed him."

He sank into the nearest chair, and when his voice came, it was pleading, almost tearful. "Please—don't do this to me! We're not enemies, we're on the same side, you're as much their victim as I am!"

I stared at him. "How do you figure that?"

"What do you suppose they think about *you*? Do you suppose they're ever going to let *you* into the club? They're snickering behind your back right now—those genteel superior little hypocrites—and calling you an uncouth little Jewboy! Don't you see, we've both been getting our asses kicked all our lives—by the same people! You can't do their dirty work for them, you can't throw me to the dogs!"

I stood up and started to the door.

He jumped to his feet and started after me. "Listen! You think I'm capable of killing somebody—so how do you know I won't— I *have* got twenty-five years on you!"

I turned to him and said, "Yes, you got up enough guts to do it once. But you'll never be able to do it again. You were right about yourself, Mike. You're not naturally a violent person."

I didn't wait for him to answer. I walked out the front door.

It was nearly midnight when I got home. Mom was waiting for me in the living room. She looked up from her book with a benign smile. For a woman who had expected her only child to be mowed down by a killer, she didn't seem particularly relieved or surprised to see me.

200

I told her everything that had happened, and then I said, "I'll call Ann now. She'll notify the DA."

Mom looked at her watch. "How long ago was it that you left his house? Half an hour, forty-five minutes? Yes, good, I think that's time enough."

That remark was completely incomprehensible to me, but I was too wrung out to give it any thought. I went to the phone and got Ann at her house. I told her the whole story, and she was silent for a long time, and finally she said, "You never know about them, do you?"

Then she told me she'd get in touch with the DA's office, and I should forget about it and get some sleep.

CHAPTER
30

BUT AN HOUR LATER I was awakened by the phone.

I answered it, and it was Ann. She sounded upset, and it takes a lot to make her sound that way. She told me that the police had just called her. They had gone to Mike Russo's house to pick him up. When nobody answered the doorbell, they broke in and found Mike lying on the floor of his kitchen, he hadn't been dead more than an hour. An empty pill bottle—some kind of sleeping pill, you could buy it without a prescription—was on the coffee table. The stereo was on, but the police report didn't say what piece was playing.

There was no note.

I hung up and stumbled out of bed and into my bathrobe. I knew I wasn't going to get back to sleep for a long time tonight. I went downstairs and found Mom in the kitchen making coffee.

I told her what had happened. I guess I didn't look too good, because she went up to me and took hold of my hand.

"Don't worry about me," I said. "I don't get guilty feelings that easy. He was a murderer, so he had to be exposed. And if that was going to make him kill himself, he would've done it sooner or later even if I *hadn't* talked to him last night."

I saw the look of relief on her face. She poured coffee for me and asked me if I wanted a cookie with it, and while I was munching it, something suddenly dawned on me.

"What are you doing down here, Mom? It's two o'clock in the morning. How come you've got coffee all ready?"

"I couldn't get to sleep. At my age, insomnia is a common—"

"Not for you, Mom. You've been sleeping like a baby for seventy-two years. You *expected* me to get that phone call, didn't you? And you knew I wouldn't be able to fall asleep again afterward. You knew what Ann would be calling about."

Mom stood up and started to brush crumbs off the table. I took hold of her wrist and eased her down into the kitchen chair. "Look at me, Mom. This is a very serious matter. We have to talk about this."

"It's so late, darling. Talking can wait until—"

"You knew ahead of time what Mike Russo would do, didn't you? You *knew* he'd kill himself if I told him he was going to be arrested again!"

She smiled softly. "You're a good detective. I always said so. One thing you're just a little bit inaccurate about though. I only *thought* I knew what Russo was going to do. There was no way I could be sure. Believe me, it was a big relief to me when I turned out—"

"Wait a second, wait a second!" I broke in, in a kind of orgy of understanding. "My God, you not only wanted me to talk to him tonight, you *manipulated* me into doing it! All those reasons I gave for going to see him—that it was my best chance of breaking him down

203

and getting him to confess and so on—you were *delighted* when I came up with those reasons, if I *hadn't* come up with them you would've come up with them yourself. And that big act you put on, telling me how worried you were about him hurting me! Actually you didn't think there was any danger at all, but you were afraid, if I didn't hear you express some concern, I'd get suspicious, I'd realize you wanted me to talk to Mike, and I might start wondering why. Damn it all, Mom, you stood by and let a man kill himself—and you made me your accomplice!"

"Did I have any choice?" she said. "Like I told you before you went to that party tonight, justice had to be done."

"Justice! He was a murderer!"

"What do you think, I'm crazy about murderers? People have a right to go on living their own lives, even if they're no-goods. Don't you follow me, Davie, it isn't justice for *him* I'm interested in, it's justice for *her*."

"Who?"

"His mother, who else? This poor old lady that sacrificed her whole life to him. Now she's in the rest home, her only pleasure is bragging to the other old ladies about her son the college professor. You want she should spend her last years feeling ashamed because of her son the murderer?"

"But he's dead. That'll give her plenty of pain."

"There's pain and pain. A boy dies young, naturally his mother feels grief. But grief and pride you can feel at the same time. You want to give her the grief and take away the pride, too?"

"The truth about the murder is bound to come out. The DA's office knows all about it—"

"The truth will come out in private maybe, people whispering rumors. But those the old lady will never hear. And in public, why should anything come out? Whatever the district attorney knows, there won't be any court case now. And he'll never give the story to the newspapers either."

"Why not? To make himself look good, to justify his arresting Mike in the first place—"

"He'll keep quiet on account of the college. Do you think the college wants there should be publicity that one professor killed another professor? Naturally not. And you told me plenty of times, the college is a very big *macher* in this town."

I could only stare at her in amazement. The smile on her face couldn't have been more serene. It simply didn't enter her mind that she might not have done the right thing.

"Look, Mom," I made one more attempt, "you're not seeing the point. Even if everybody is better off because Mike Russo killed himself, *you* never had the right to make that decision. You just can't take the law into your own hands. Do you understand what I'm saying?"

"How couldn't I understand?"

"Well, then, will you promise me—your solemn promise, Mom—you'll never do anything like this again."

She reached over and patted me on the cheek. "You're so upset about this. Only stop being upset, and I'll promise."

I wasn't too pleased at the way she said this, but sometimes you have to settle for what you can get.

CHAPTER
31

MOM'S PREDICTIONS TURNED OUT to be completely accurate. The next morning, when I got to the office, Ann told me officially that the district attorney didn't intend to make any public accusations in connection either with Mike Russo's or Stuart Bellamy's death. Since there was no defendant to put on trial, the case was now closed, the official theory being that Russo had taken an accidental overdose of pills and that Bellamy had fallen from a chair, while reaching for a book at the top of his bookshelf, and struck his head against a paperweight that was lying on his desk.

So Mom had been right about Mesa Grande College. Her long experience of life had taught her what a big *macher* can do.

At dinner that night, while she seduced me with her special roast beef and Yorkshire pudding, Mom broke two pieces of news to me. First, she had called up the airline and made reservations to go back to New York the next morning.

"But what's your hurry?" I said. "You've only been

here a week. Has it been that boring for you? I realize I didn't give you more than one murder—"

"I'm going home because you know what next Friday is? It's Passover. I have to get back in time to start getting ready for the seder."

"You're having a lot of people?"

"The synagogue is having a lot of people. A couple hundred. And five of us are doing the food. My job is the chopped liver."

Chopped liver for two hundred people! It was more than the human imagination could encompass.

"And also," Mom added, "I have to start advertising my furniture for sale."

"You want to sell your furniture, Mom? All that old stuff that you bought when you and Dad first got married?"

"Old junk is what it is. If I make a couple hundred dollars out of it, I'll be lucky. And those pictures—the English landscapes and the Roman ruins—for fifty-five years they've been boring me to death. I'm hoping I can talk some garbageman into carting them away for nothing."

"But why do you want to get rid of all your things, after all these years?"

"You don't think I'm paying good money to ship all those *schmattes* out here, do you? There's very nice furniture for sale in this town, I've been looking around."

Finally I caught on. I was on my feet immediately, hugging her. "Enough, enough already!" she pushed me away.

Later I asked her why she had changed her mind. What made her decide to settle in Mesa Grande after all?

She gave one of her shrugs. "Who knows?" she said. "Maybe you convinced me this isn't such an uncivilized place. Not so civilized as New York City, naturally, but not from the cavemen either. You got a synagogue, you got a college, you got a place to play bridge, you got a supermarket with matzo ball soup, you got a mountain that don't look too bad when there aren't any clouds. You even got some interesting murders."

"When is it going to be, Mom? How long before you'll be coming back here?"

"I'll need maybe five weeks. The first of May, does this sound like a convenient date?"

"It sounds perfect. And which bedroom are you going to want? It won't be any trouble for me to switch around if you prefer—"

"Bedrooms!" She gave a snort. "What do you think, I'll be living with you in this house?"

"Well, naturally I assumed—"

"Stop assuming, thank you. For thirty-four years of my life I lived with a man, and also for some of those years with a growing boy—your father and you, that is. For thirty-four years I did all the cooking and washed all the clothes and cleaned the toilet bowls daily. It was very nice, I was happy to do it—but for the *last* twenty years, I'm living alone, I'm taking care of the food and clothes and toilet bowls for only one person, and it suits me nicely. So if you're looking for a woman to do for you what I used to do, please go on looking, I'll even give you a little help if you want—but excuse me, *I* don't volunteer. I'm in the market for a nice one-bedroom condominium, and the prices out here, if you go by New York standards, aren't bad."

"My God, you've been *pricing* them already?"

"And also, keep your eyes open for a nice used car. A little foreign model maybe with four seats in it? One thing I found out while I was visiting you. In this town of yours, since nobody was ever smart enough to build a subway, people can't get around without a car."

"I didn't know you could drive a car."

"This is another thing I'll be doing in the next five weeks. I'll take lessons."

She laughed and told me to close my mouth or I'd get a fly down my throat. It was what she used to say to me all the time when I was a kid.

The next morning I saw Mom off on the plane. She put her arms around me and gave me one of her quick businesslike kisses. "All right, all right, good-bye is unnecessary. I'm back in only five weeks. I'm practically not going away at all."

She turned quickly, and her dumpy little figure disappeared down the ramp.

Driving home, I realized that today was Tuesday. I'd be seeing Marcia tonight. We'd be going to the movies. The new Robert Redford was in town, and while I personally could take him or leave him Marcia was crazy about him. She found him as beautiful as a poem.

Talking about poems, my heart leaped up. I realized how nice it would be to spend the evening with a woman who nods her head at you while you talk and hangs on your every word.

EPILOGUE

My darling son Davie,

I'm sitting here in the airplane, flying back to New York, and writing to you this letter. And even while I'm writing it I know I'm not going to send it.

For a couple of days now I'm arguing about this inside myself. Should I tell you the truth, or should I keep it strictly to myself? On the one hand, is it good for my health I should keep it inside myself like a bottle? On the other hand, if I tell you the truth, don't I know what you'll do with it?

So what I decided is, I'll write this all down on paper, get it out of my system, and then I'll throw it away.

What I'm referring to is who killed the professor.

No, it isn't exactly that I told you any lies again. Everything I explained to you two days ago was true. My chain of reasoning didn't have anything wrong with it. It was a beautiful chain of reasoning. But even while I was putting it together, I felt funny about it. I couldn't pretend there weren't a few bits and pieces which just wouldn't fall into place.

What I finally realized is, these bits and pieces don't contradict my earlier conclusions. What they show me is, there are other conclusions, too. The ones I can't ever tell you about.

Probably you could work them out by yourself, if you went over in your mind everything that happened in the last week.

Anyway, the point is that Mike Russo did everything I told you he did. No, excuse me, almost everything. The one thing he didn't do was to kill Bellamy.

He said so himself, you remember? He said he got to Bellamy's house, he went into his living room, he was all ready to kill him, but somebody beat him to it. You didn't believe him. For an hour or so I didn't believe him either. Why should we believe him, a man that told as many lies as he did and definitely, except for one small technicality, was a murderer?

But on this one matter he was telling the truth. Once I was ready to consider this possibility, all those bits and pieces clicked into place.

First of all, when you finally got Luis Vallejos to admit he went out to Bellamy's house, what did he say he did? He said he walked into Bellamy's living room, found his body, started to run out in a panic, bumped into something and lost his earring, which rolled under one of the bookcases. This happened, Vallejos said, at maybe ten minutes after eight, just before the police officers got to the scene of the crime.

So let's think about this fact along with another one. Samantha Fletcher, when she had dinner with Vallejos between six-thirty and seven-forty that night, thought there was something different about him. "His face was different," only she couldn't put her finger on why.

I'm asking myself, could the reason be that Vallejos was wearing only one of his earrings during that dinner?

Could he maybe have lost the other earring earlier? Could it have rolled under Bellamy's bookcase before six-thirty?

In other words, could Vallejos have gone to Bellamy's house not after but before he met Fletcher at the restaurant?

Second of all, at the end of their dinner together, Vallejos left Fletcher to go to the washroom, he always went there to give his hair a combing. A few minutes later he came back, and he was looking—I'm using Fletcher's own words—"as if he'd seen a ghost." Then he announced he had to go somewhere immediately, but he would be at Fletcher's house by ten o'clock.

So again I'm asking myself—what was Vallejos going to do which he expected wouldn't take him longer than a couple of hours? He was going to Bellamy's house, he told

211

us, to try and talk Bellamy into giving him a passing grade on his exam. But how could he be sure such a talk would be short enough so he could get to Fletcher's house by ten? It's a twenty-five-minute drive to Bellamy's house from downtown Mesa Grande—and Bellamy might delay Vallejos when he got there—or Bellamy might not be home, and Vallejos might have to wait for him. A lot of maybes, but none of them stopped Vallejos from promising Fletcher he'd be at her house by ten.

Could it be that Vallejos knew for sure he wouldn't be talking to Bellamy when he got to his house that night—because he knew Bellamy was already dead? Could it be that Vallejos' real reason for going there was to search for the earring he dropped when he was in that house earlier in the evening?

Could it be that the "ghost" Vallejos saw in the restaurant washroom was his own face in the mirror, minus the earring?

Third of all, Vallejos told us he ran out of Bellamy's house so quick after finding the body that he didn't even shut the door behind him. But you and the police, when you got there only a few minutes later, found that door shut tight and locked.

Why was Vallejos confused about this? Could it be he didn't actually run out of that house just before the police got there, because on that occasion he never even had time to go into it? Could it be he heard a car coming, your car, while he was still on the porch steps walking up to the front door, which meant that he had to run away before he had a chance to go inside and search for his earring?

Could it be that Vallejos was remembering an earlier visit to the house, at six o'clock or close to it, at which time he did forget to shut the door behind him?

We shouldn't forget what Russo told you. He found the front door halfway open when he got to the house at seven-fifteen, he walked into the house by this door, and when he left in a big hurry a little while later he slammed the door behind him.

You see what it proves, this business of the door? Vallejos left it open when he ran out—Russo slammed it behind him when he ran out—you and the police found it shut tight. Which means that Vallejos was in that house before Russo, that his story about being in there at eight-ten is a lie.

212

Fourthly, Vallejos' sister told you he took her car and left his parents' home at five-fifteen Wednesday afternoon. Fletcher told you Vallejos arrived at the restaurant at six-thirty. It doesn't take an hour, fifteen minutes to get from the Vallejos house to the Seafood Grotto. So where was the boy all this time?

Fifthly, when Vallejos described for you the scene of the murder, he made a little mistake. He said, "I went up to the phone, but I didn't pick up the receiver, I left it on the hook." But Russo, when he discovered the body at seven-fifteen, took the receiver off the hook and dropped the phone on the floor. This was what you and the police officers saw a little over an hour later, when you went into Bellamy's house.

In other words, Vallejos could never have seen the phone sitting in its place, with the receiver on the hook, unless he was inside that room before Russo got there.

And the only explanation for this is, he killed Bellamy himself.

So here's my theory about what happened. It isn't a theory, it's the truth, because nothing else explains everything. Luis Vallejos wanted to make one last try at talking Bellamy into changing his grade, and he went out to Bellamy's house for that reason—but he did it between five forty-five and six o'clock, just before his dinner with Fletcher, not at eight-ten, right after his dinner with Fletcher.

Bellamy let the boy in, and he reacted to the apologies exactly the way you'd expect. He sneered. He laughed. He told the boy to get out of there. Maybe he even said he'd call the police and report that the boy came there to threaten him. Maybe he even turned away from Vallejos and started to the phone.

Luis Vallejos has a hot temper. Even a cool temper could heat up with Bellamy's type treatment. The boy grabbed the first weapon he could get his hands on—it happened to be the paperweight that was shaped like an open book—and hit Bellamy on the back of the head. Bellamy went down, and the boy was sure he was dead. It wasn't premeditated murder. At worst maybe it was manslaughter. A good lawyer could maybe get him off with temporary insanity. But who was going to believe his story?

He tried to wipe his fingerprints off the paperweight, and then he ran out of the house. He drove straight to the restaurant where Fletcher was waiting for him. At the end of the dinner he noticed his earring was missing, guessed where it was, and drove out to Bellamy's house again hoping he could find this evidence against him before somebody found the body. But the police got there too soon, and he had to run away.

And in the meantime what about Bellamy? Head wounds are tricky, like the assistant district attorney told you at the beginning of this case. Bellamy was unconscious for an hour or more, bleeding inside, probably dying—but he wasn't dead yet. When Russo got to the house at seven-fifteen, there was still enough life in Bellamy so he could make "gurgling noises."

Then he died, and Russo put the book into his hand, knocked over the telephone, made his meshuga phone call, and turned the case into a big mishmash for everybody.

So that's what happened, Davie. But knowing what happened isn't enough. I also had to decide what to do about it. I decided, naturally, by using my logic, which is the only thing that makes human beings different from the lowly animals. Meaning that I asked myself one question: If Luis Vallejos goes to jail, what's the result?

A nineteen-year-old boy—who was never in trouble with the police before, who studies hard in school, loves to read books, and maybe has a wonderful future ahead of him— loses twenty, thirty, years of his life. Not to mention what happens to young boys like him when they're in prison, as we're all familiar with from shows on television.

The boy's mother and father and his brothers and sisters that love him and all their lives have sacrificed to give him an education get their hearts broken.

Samantha Fletcher, if the boy goes on trial, testifies in the courtroom, and her affair comes out into the open. So she's fired from her job, and she has to give up the teaching profession.

Mike Russo's mother, in the old people's home in Washington Heights, reads about the Vallejos boy's trial in the newspapers. She finds out what her son was really like, and so do the other old people. Another heart is broken.

And why does all this happen? Because of a no-good who got pleasure from kicking people that were weaker than him. All right, I know I said to you once that even no-goods have a right to live their lives, that nobody should get away with committing murder. But was it murder, what this boy did? Or was it a fit of temporary insanity, when this no-good said things to him that nobody should have to listen to? Is

214

he a murderer, or is he a confused frightened boy that lost his temper, and everything went black, and he didn't have any idea what he was doing?

So my next move is obvious, isn't it? No move. Nothing. I keep my mouth shut.

You see any flaws in my logic?

There aren't any flaws. Even so, if there's one thing I'm positive about in this world, it's this—logic or not, you won't go along with what I've decided to do.

I can hear it now, in my imagination, what you'll say to me. How I've got no right to take the law into my own hands. How no individual person, especially an uneducated old lady, should put herself above the rules of society. How it's about time I learned that it isn't up to me to see to it that justice is done. And so on and so forth. I love you like only a mother can love her son, Davie darling, but frankly I'm not crazy about hearing all that foolishness from you.

Not that I'm blaming you for it, you understand. At an early age you made up your mind you should be a policeman. God knows it wasn't what I advised you to do, but since when do children take the advice of their parents? So you became a policeman, and they taught you to think in a certain way, and now you're stuck with it.

And the way a policeman thinks, a man who commits a murder, even a boy who commits a murder, has to be punished for it. It's too bad if innocent people get punished along with him, this is just how it has to be.

In other words, if I was foolish enough that I told you the truth about the Vallejos boy, you wouldn't let five minutes go by until you told it all to your boss and to the district attorney. The case would be reopened, evidence would be dug up, and pretty soon everybody who's happy now would be miserable all over again.

Including you, by the way, because you're a sensitive kindhearted person and you'd feel terrible about what you did.

This I can't allow to happen. For the sake of all those people and for your sake, too.

Which is why you'll never see this letter. It goes into a trash can as soon as the airplane lands in LaGuardia airport. Even so, I'm glad I wrote it. Already I'm feeling better. Like a big load was lifted off my mind.

It's only five weeks before I'll see you again, Davie

215

darling. What a pleasure to look forward to! And by that time, no doubt, you'll have an entirely new murder that you can tell me about.

With love, like always,
Mom